HIDDEN IDENTITIES

Tara worked as an artist in London, but she also owned a vineyard in Devon. Driving back home to the West Country one night she was involved in an annoying encounter with the driver of a black Saab. Then, on arriving home, she was amazed to meet the same man again — and this time he had the audacity to kiss her! There was an obvious attraction between her and this mysterious man, but they both had secrets they couldn't share.

Books by Patricia Freer
in the Linford Romance Library:

WHEN TOMORROW COMES
CHARMING DECEPTION
A THING OF BEAUTY
TWISTED STRANDS
WIFE WANTED

PATRICIA FREER

◆

HIDDEN
IDENTITIES

Complete and Unabridged

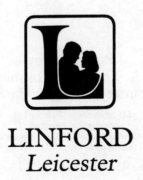

LINFORD
Leicester

First published in Great Britain

First Linford Edition
published 2002

British Library CIP Data

Freer, Patricia
  Hidden identities.—Large print ed.—
  Linford romance library
  1. Love stories
  2. Large type books
  I. Title
  823.9′14 [F]

  ISBN 0–7089–9773–2

Published by
F. A. Thorpe (Publishing)
Anstey, Leicestershire

Set by Words & Graphics Ltd.
Anstey, Leicestershire
Printed and bound in Great Britain by
T. J. International Ltd., Padstow, Cornwall

This book is printed on acid-free paper

1

Oh, come on Tara. One more night in town won't hurt you. It's been a great exhibition, better than either of us dreamed. I'll ring Jo and we'll take you for a celebration meal.'

'No, really, Derek.' Tara smiled to soften the refusal. 'It's tempting, honestly it is, but I'm itching to get back. You know what I'm like — a real country mouse at heart.'

'Some mouse.' Derek looked admiringly at the sophisticated girl standing before him. 'More of a glamour puss, I'd say.'

Tara chuckled with him and gave him a quick peck on his cheek. 'Thanks,' she said softly. 'Thank Jo for me, too — you've both been terrific.'

It was true. Derek and his wife had been a tremendous help to her, not just at this exhibition, but over the whole of the last few years. If it was Tara's skill that had made her an artist of national repute, it was Derek's careful management that had put her name so firmly on the map.

They had reached their parked cars and Tara said, 'I hate to leave you, but you know this isn't my favourite scene. If I had to spend any more time with glitzy people, I think I'd scream. The prospect of another cocktail, or one more smile at a potential buyer, fills me with horror.'

'I was only suggesting a quiet dinner.'

'Oh. I know — and don't think I'm not grateful, but you can see I'm so keen to get back to Devon that I haven't even changed. My case is in the car boot. If I go now I'll be back before dark.'

'OK. I can see you're desperate to shake off the dust of the big city.' He patted her shoulder forgivingly and opened the car door for her.

'Get back to your old grass roots then — and get busy on those canvases, ready for our next exhibition.'

'I will.' Tara waved from the car window as she filtered out into the traffic, but after that she was forced to concentrate on manoeuvring her way through the busy streets. It was a relief when she was finally able to join the motorway for the West Country.

The M4, Tara found, was relatively uncrowded. Pressing her high-heeled foot hard down on the accelerator, she watched the speedometer rise, feeling a sense of exhilaration at the sound of the wind whistling past. She enjoyed driving fast and was anxious to get home.

Goodbye London, hello Tamary Hollow, she thought contentedly, back to my real self, and time to do what I really want. In her mind's eye she pictured her cottage. On such a sunny evening the white walls would be shining and the thick paned windows glinting.

How incredibly lucky she had been to find such a gem of a property. When financial success had made it possible for her to buy her own home it had been a wonderful bonus to find, not just a delightful storybook cottage for sale in a rural paradise, but a cottage with a rundown vineyard attached.

Impatiently, Tara flashed her head-lights as she was forced to slow down behind a black Saab. The driver seemed to think that the third lane was for cruising. 'Oh, move over,' she said aloud but, to her annoyance, the big car made no attempt to let her pass.

'Road hog!' Fuming, she kept close behind him, ready to sweep by as soon as he let her. To her annoyance, he began instead, to pull away and put more distance between them. Glancing at her speedometer, Tara gasped a little and eased up on the throttle. 'Be like that,' she said to the back of the disappearing car, 'I'm not idiotic enough to try racing on the motorway.'

But the incident annoyed her a little, a smudge on her clear horizon.

She had driven a further twenty miles

before she saw the signs for her usual service station stop. Since she took this journey at least five times a year she had developed the habit of stopping to fill up just before Bristol. Slowing gradually, she eased into the slip road and drew alongside the lines of parked cars, finally nosing her silver hatchback into a space near the restaurant.

After getting out of the car, she leaned again across the passenger seat to reach her bag which had fallen down the other side. The short, tight skirt and sheer stockings she wore were not the best garb for this manoeuvre but no-one was close enough to see. Or so she thought until she lost her balance stepping backward and nearly went sprawling! Then, a strong grip caught and steadied her. Tara, furious at her own clumsiness, said 'Thanks. I would have fallen without you to hold me up.'

'Yes you would have. Driving in unsuitable shoes is something only a stupid woman would do.'

The man let her go so abruptly she

almost fell anyway.

Tara gasped, twisted round and would have responded to this unmannerly stranger in kind except that he gave her no change to speak again. He had already strode away and was not looking back.

Robbed of the chance to defend herself, Tara looked fumingly after him but he was stepping into his vehicle. And it was the final irritation, in an annoying incident, to see that he was the driver of the black Saab!

As he eased the big car towards the exit road, from its window, infuriatingly, a hand waved in nonchalant farewell.

What a maddening episode! Momentarily Tara was fuming, but was too sensible to dwell for long on her injured pride. Better spirits soon prevailed and she was able to smile about it as she picked up her bag and made for the restaurant. Whoever he was, she reflected, he certainly had a nerve. And, although she burned with the desire to say a few scathing words about his rude and sexist remark, she was clearly never to have the opportunity so all that was left to do was dismiss the matter from her mind.

Sipping her coffee, she watched the people. Faces had lately become of intense interest to her and there was plenty of scope in the motorway cafe to spot interesting planes and contours. The artist in Tara longed to draw the thin, hollowed face of an elderly woman, or to capture the rounded bloom of the big-eyed child at the next table. Absorbed, the irritation of the earlier episode completely faded.

★ ★ ★

It was hours later when Tara eventually reached Tamary Hollow and the evening sunshine had merged into darkness. As always when she arrived back, she felt a stir of excitement. A little shiver of pleased anticipation swept through her as she unlocked her front door with a large, old-fashioned key and flung her bag onto the couch.

Kneeling by the big granite fireplace she struck a match and lit the fire. Although Spring it was still cold and a fire was part of the ambience she liked to create. Savouring the moment, she poured a glass of wine into one of her favourite crystal glasses, and slipped a soothing tape into the recorder. At last she could relax.

It was vitally important to Tara that she should remain anonymous in the village.

As a child she had watched her father ruin his artistic brilliance because of too early fame. He had not been able to cope with it, had turned to drink, and become a dilettante, eventually leaving his family. Because of this Tara, as her reputation grew, had vowed to tell no-one about her growing success. From then on she had lived two separate existences, and friends from one knew nothing about the other.

As she went to draw the curtains she saw that the moon had risen, sending shafts of light across the garden path. Tempted, she went quickly to the door to stand under the trellissed arch of the porch, breathing in the delicious smell of early honeysuckle.

The tap tap of her heels rang loudly and incongruously on the path. She was certainly not dressed for the country but she didn't want to stop and change now. As she opened the gate she wondered, ruefully, if she wasn't becoming a shade too interested in her vineyard.

The previous owners had been defeated by lack of money and the vagaries of the English climate. They had cut their losses and moved on.

Tara loved wine but had decided to let the land return to nature. Meeting Tom, her present manager, at the village inn had changed her mind — he was keen to restart the winery and she had been fired by his enthusiasm.

Last year, her three acres had produced 5000 bottles of good quality white wine. This year, Tom was keen to try a new variety of wine, and she had enthusiastically agreed.

Of one thing she was certain, her interest was in the challenge of the product, not in its potential profit and she was determined to keep it that way.

The gate creaked a little and, as she stepped out on to the paving stones, Tara realised, too late, that she should have carried a torch rather than a glass of wine. The moon had retreated behind a cloud and she felt a chill, as though cobwebs traced themselves down her spine. It was ridiculous, she told herself, to be afraid in the country. She'd walked through her garden and into the vineyard many times before at night. So, what was making her feel so tense?

Small, night animals rustled in the hedge and the slight breeze shifted the shadows eerily. Turning her head, she thought she saw a movement that was more than a branch shifting in the wind — yes, she was sure of it! The dark bulk, the black outline, between her and the gate, was that of a man — a large man.

Taking a step backward and opening her mouth to cry out she recalled, in panic, that she could not even run in the clothes she wore — if running became necessary! Yet when a hand shot out and covered her mouth she was more astonished and outraged than frightened. The fear came when she found herself in an iron grip. He seemed a huge figure, big enough to blot out the light, big enough to tower over her, tall as she was. When he spoke, although it was in an undertone, there was an elusively familiar quality about his voice that Tara could not place. 'Don't scream,' he said quickly, deeply. 'I'm sorry to have frightened you, but what are you doing, wandering about here all by yourself in the middle of the night?'

'What am I doing?' she hissed, as soon as his hand had left her mouth. 'It's you who should be explaining yourself. I've got a perfect right to be here. I live here.' His tight grasp of her had not loosened and she struggled to get free, saying, 'Let go of me!'

The man continued to hold her and, as Tara gazed unbelievingly up at him, the moon emerged from the clouds and illuminated his face. He was in his thirties, dark bearded and black-browed. There was a gaunt intensity about his look.

'Do you often take evening walks in the country dressed like that?' His eyes swept disapprovingly down over her. 'And with a glass in your hand?' he added with a look of contempt.

Tara said nothing. Her thoughts raced. Although hot, defensive words rose to her lips, she did not utter them. Neither did she move again. Still clutching her glass, she stood transfixed, watching the changing expressions on his dark face. He had allowed his hands to drop away but they still stood, chest to chest.

He took in the smoothness of her cheeks, the green, black-lashed eyes and the slightly parted lips, only inches from his.

In quite a different tone he whispered, 'You're beautiful. It's been a long time since I've seen anything like you.' His voice was husky, his face that of a man in a dream and his hands came up again and took hold of her shoulders.

Tara, who recognised desire when she saw it, cast about for words or ways to save herself, aware that neither screaming nor running would be of any use, for he could stop her effortlessly. Strangely she did neither. She could not even try, because a strange lethargy was creeping through her body.

Irrelevantly, she noticed the rough texture of his hands as he took hold of her face and, like a man in a dream, brought his mouth down on hers. She never even heard her glass falling because, as he pressed his lips to hers, she became conscious of his hunger, a hunger more fierce and demanding than she'd ever known before. Her ears pounded with an incessant drumming that grew louder and all she could think of, despairingly, was trying to prevent them both from falling.

When he raised his head his breathing came raggedly and his eyes, as they looked down on her, were dazed. The terror he saw in her face seemed to bring sanity back to him. He let her go abruptly and stepped back, shaking his head as though to clear it. He saw her put up a finger to touch her lips and quickly extended a hand in mute apology, taking it down, in a defeated way, when she recoiled from the contact.

'Why?' She asked it loudly, urgently. 'Why treat a strange woman like that? You're not some crazy kid — these aren't city streets.'

'I'm sorry. Isn't that enough? Drop it — please.' His angry impatience was overriding his shame, but she was not to be deterred.

'No, it isn't enough. It's easy just to apologise — but I want an explanation. What are you doing here?'

He made an impatient movement but did not speak.

Tara stood tall, her chin up, waiting, but when the silence had continued too long for comfort the moody moon sailed out of sight again and she was belatedly conscious of feeling cold. She drew her thin, tight-fitting jacket around her, unable to suppress a shiver. As though forced into speech, he said, 'That's partly it — the way you look.'

'I see. You mean you're one of those male chauvinists who say a woman asked for it because she looks attractive. I despise that kind of thinking.'

His air of forcefulness was restored in the sudden short laugh he gave. Face totally transformed, the dour look chased out by a grin which made small crinkles around his eyes, he said admiringly, 'You've certainly got spirit. Here you are, totally in my power, alone, helpless, and you're daring to tell me you despise me.'

Tara snapped back at him, 'Keep to the point. Why were you here — and why did you kiss me like that?'

'You reminded me of someone — someone I don't like very much — someone I haven't seen for quite a while.' He seemed to think this was sufficient explanation.

'And this someone,' Tara pursued, when he paused, 'is usually unlucky enough to get the full brunt of your feelings, is she?'

'No.' It was a sharp denial but his face was stony, his voice expressionless as he went on. 'There's another reason. I haven't seen a woman — I haven't been near anyone . . .'

He halted and tailed off lamely but Tara thought she got the gist of it and said sarcastically, 'I suppose you've been on a desert island for years.' Something crept back into his eyes and Tara judged it wisest to go.

Carefully, with a brief, 'Excuse me, I'm getting cold,' she sidestepped around him, towards the gate and the lighted path. To her infinite relief he made no attempt to stop her.

It was not until she stood in the comparative safety of her own doorstep that she had the courage to call back to the silent, unmoving figure. 'You have no right to be here. Please leave this property — now.'

'Don't worry, I'm going.' He finally stirred and began, unhurriedly to move away. Determined to see that he left, Tara stood, bathed in the pool of light from behind her. She wanted to make sure that she saw him actually leave her territory. Nevertheless it was only when she heard a car engine start up from the road in front of the cottage that she allowed her whole body to relax, and realised how tensely she had been holding herself.

Craning her neck she saw the car go by and realised at last why his voice had had an elusively familiarity. He was the driver of the black Saab.

2

Tara awoke next day to brilliant sunshine. Last night's incident was no more than a small cloud on her horizon. Ships that pass in the night, she decided, and was glad that this one had passed so quickly.

Stretching luxuriously she revelled in the bright comfort of her bedroom. Elation filled her at the thought of spending the long Summer ahead, at her beloved Tamary Hollow.

Minutes later she stood under a stinging shower, her chestnut hair unpinned and loose around her shoulders. It felt as though the sluicing water was washing away the tensions of London life and the days of being on show.

Pulling on jeans and a shirt, she towelled her hair roughly and went downstairs. Tara's kitchen had all the labour-saving gadgets but she had taken care to retain the cottage atmosphere. She was a good cook but being a working artist was her first priority and that meant efficiently streamlining the domestic side of her life.

Soon the fragrance of fresh coffee began to fill the air and Tara leaned against a pine dresser sipping orange juice and sighing contentedly. It was good to recall the success of her recent exhibition but today she had promised herself time relaxing in the vineyard. Some hard physical work would be exhilarating.

After that she was longing to begin another portrait. She recalled Derek's words before the exhibition.

'Being a landscape painter has made you rich, famous and successful. Why do you want to change direction now?'

And although she had smiled, she had still included several portraits in the show. They had been much admired and quickly sold, so her experiment had been completely justified, thank goodness.

Her thoughts still on portraits, an eminently paintable face came into her mind; a dark, handsome face with piercing grey eyes, strong planes, a sensuous mouth, but with a hint of bitterness in the expression. Did she imagine a haunting sadness behind the grey eyes? In any case it was a face of contradictions and ambiguities, with the look of an Elizabethan buccaneer, an adventurer who yet longed for home and shelter.

It was a distinct shock to look out of the window and see the owner of the face once again tresspassing on her property!

He was standing in the courtyard, in the centre of a small group of the vineyard workers. Taller than any of them, he was unmistakeably the mystery man of the previous night. What on earth was he doing there? The ships in the night had, apparently, not passed after all!

Her breakfast forgotten, Tara stepped out into the warm, Spring morning. As she emerged from her garden gate, the men greeted her.

'Hi, Tara. Good to see you back.' That was Tom, her young vineyard manager.

'Hello, Miss Cresswell. How was London?' Jan, an elderly pensioner, one of the part-time workers.

She acknowledged them with a smile, acutely aware of the dominating presence amongst them. 'It was fine. But it's nice to be home again.'

From underneath her thick lashes she saw that he was staring at her intently. Had it been only hours ago that he had held her in a tight grip, his mouth pressed to hers? For one earth-stopping moment she was only conscious of the two of them, everything else retreated, as though out of focus; the murmur of the other's voices sounding as from a vast distance. Then, thankfully, the world righted itself again.

She turned to Tom to ask him what

the plans were for the day. He had been giving the others orders and they were starting to drift off to begin work. Soon, only three of them remained; the stranger, Tara and Tom.

Tom said 'This is Ben Lavalle — he's looking for casual work. I've taken him on, since we need someone to help with the new vines.'

Ben. So that was his name! It was too homey, too comfortable for such an enigmatic presence. She waited to see whether he would mention their strange meeting in front of Tom, but he had shaded his eyes with a hand held up against the dazzle of the morning sun and she realised that he had not recognised her.

Slowly, disbelievingly he said, 'Surely — it can't be . . . the girl in the garden — in the moonlight?'

The deep voice was incredulous as he took in her cotton shirt, and faded jeans, hair swinging loose and straight in the sun.

'Oh, but it is, Mr Lavalle. It's also, if

you recall, the girl at the motorway service station.'

Her voice was clipped as she added, 'I don't know how you've got the cheek to come back here.'

'As Tom says, I'm looking for work,' he answered easily, 'which is why,' he continued, 'I'd like to meet the owner of the vineyard — if he's available.'

Tom, looked embarrassed, was about to speak, but was stopped by a gesture from Tara.

'He,' she stressed sarcastically, 'happens to be a woman. I'm Tara Cresswell and I own Tamary Vineyards.'

Instead of looking confounded as she hoped he might, Ben's lips curved in a small smile.

'Is that so? Then I realise now why I had to come back — I knew, last night, that you were somehow rather . . . ' he paused, as though hunting for the right word, then with an intimately lowered voice he murmured, ' . . . different.'

The word was innocuous but the cool, grey eyes and the look that went with it, deliberately flattered. Tara averted her own eyes, her glance falling on his hands, noting that, although well shaped they were hard and rough. Unease stirred in the pit of her stomach as memories returned of the encounter in the moonlight.

Tom, sensing the tension between them, spoke anxiously. 'I'm sorry, Tara. I thought . . . '

'It's all right, Tom, of course we need extra help. Find Mr Lavalle something to do, will you. I'm going over to the bottom field.'

Pointedly she walked away, hoping she had put the over-bearing stranger in his place. Her optimism was short lived. Within moments he had fallen easily into step with her, matching his long stride to hers. Angrily, she burst out, 'Why are you following me? You're supposed to be . . . '

He interupted coolly. 'I'm exactly where I'm supposed to be. Tom asked me to measure for wire and stakes for the new vines.'

His keen eyes scanned the fields, as he asked abruptly, 'How long have you been here?'

Tara answered reluctantly, 'Four years.'

'You've done well. The vines are healthy and the land looks good. What were your production figures last year?'

Tara gasped, unable to believe her ears. 'Look,' her voice cracked with irritation, 'what's it got to do with you? It's my business. I don't need any interference.'

They faced each other. Ben's shabby jeans covered long, lean legs, well muscled thighs and a taut, flat stomach. His sleeveless black T-shirt was old and torn and provided scant covering for his powerful chest. Tara noted the odd pallor of his skin, unusual for a man whose physique was patently suited to the outdoors. There was a disturbing quality about him — so much so, that she wished he would go away and leave her alone.

Ignoring her outburst he said, 'Tom

says you're going to plant this area with a new variety. I'm not sure that's a good idea. The climate is too damp.' He looked at her, his face serious and preoccupied.

'What do you know about it? If I need advice, I can get it.'

His voice sharpened. 'Look, I know what I'm talking about. It would be a waste to ruin all this.' He indicated the green fields and budding vines. 'It's a wonderful spot — you could work miracles here.' His arm came to rest lightly on her shoulder.

Tara was unprepared for the strangeness of the feeling which flowed through her. She felt his will imposing on hers. She stepped quickly back. 'I think we should start work. It's getting late.'

His hand dropped immediately. 'Just as you say. It'll keep, anyway.'

For the rest of the day, Tara worked hard in the fields, savouring the hot sunshine. Ben Lavalle, she thrust firmly out of her mind.

In the late afternoon, she and Tom returned to the cottage and planned the work of the next few days over a cup of tea.

'I've enjoyed today, Tom. You don't know what a relief it is to get back to Tamary Hollow after a spell in London. I feel a new woman. Just one day and I'm ready to start work again.' Tom glanced at her curiously and she added, hastily, deliberately vague, 'You know, getting ready for the next trip. Not yet of course.'

Tom nodded understandingly. No-one, least of all he, knew she was a highly successful artist, and she intended to keep it that way, encouraging the rumour that her London visits were sales trips. The general opinion amongst the village gossips was that she bought and sold antiques. They had no inkling that she was the famous painter, 'Tamara'.

Tom sipped his tea thoughtfully. 'The new man, Ben, he seems to know about vines. Wanted to know where our bottling plant was — I showed him the shed at the back.'

He snorted in recollection. 'He didn't seem very impresed!'

They both collapsed with laughter.

'Well,' Tara said, her voice spurting with giggles, 'I don't suppose he was. Bottling plant indeed! Did you tell him, it's all hand bottled here?'

'No, I didn't. I thought he'd find out soon enough, if he stays that long. Seems like a bit of a wanderer.'

Tara looked up sharply. 'Did he say he was leaving soon?'

'No — he didn't say much about himself at all. Asked questions most of the time. He's got quite a persuasive way with him.'

Tom carried his cup over to the sink.

'I think he probably will stay a while. He certainly seems mightily interested in this place.'

'Hmm.' Tara was non committal. 'Let's tidy up outside, Tom, and then I'll call it a day. I'm quite tired.'

Later that evening, sitting cross-legged on the rug in front of the granite fireplace, she watched the logs leap into crackling flame and listened absently to soothing music. The face of the stranger still haunted her artist's imagination and the urge to give it concrete expression was strong.

Absorbed in her reflections, she was oblivious to the discreet click as the tape ended. For a moment she thought that the chime of the doorbell was part of the music, until the silence which followed told her that someone was at the front door. Frowning, she hesitated. She didn't feel at all like visitors, but ignoring them would not work; her lights unmistakeably announced that she was at home. The bell sounded again, more insistently and she got up and went into the hall.

As she reached it, the front door yielded to outside pressure, swinging open to reveal Ben Lavalle, some books in one hand, a bottle of wine in the other.

Neither of them spoke for a moment until he said lightly, 'Who is it tonight

— the girl in the motorway or the vineyard owner? At present I'd like to talk to the latter and it looks as though I've got it right.' His smile was wide, his dark grey eyes humorous as he appraised her tall, willowy figure in its casual track suit.

Tara noted, with curiosity, that the cream sweater slung carelessly over his shoulder, was expensive cashmere, and his leather shoes were hand-made.

Why was a man like this working as a casual labourer, she wondered.

Without being asked he had already crossed the threshold and was holding out the wine bottle.

'A peace offering from an uninvited guest,' he said, handing it to her. Then, exaggeratedly sniffing, he said, 'Your supper smells good — are you eating all alone?'

The suggestion in this innocent question was blatant and Tara had to laugh. 'More of a gate-crasher than a guest, I'd say. What would you do if I had any visitors?'

'I'd come another time — of course. But you haven't, have you? I know you're alone tonight.' He had already walked past her into the firelit sitting room and, as he looked round, she watched his reaction.

He said, 'Did you do this?'

'I furnished it, of course, but the beams, the fireplace . . . ' she gestured around the cosy room with pride, 'were already here, came with the original cottage.'

'I'm impressed. It's delightful. Obviously getting it like this must have cost a fortune but you've stamped personality and style onto natural beauty. You've added something that makes it . . . ' the words seemed to give him trouble.

'Home?' Tara supplied.

'Yes. That's it — simple. But I couldn't think of it . . . home!'

'It's not so difficult.'

'Not for you, perhaps, but . . . ' Ben stopped, the enthusiasm dying from his expression. He changed the subject. 'Look — these books

— they're on viticulture . . . there's a section here . . . ' Tara watched as his long fingers flipped quickly through the pages, noticing his well-manicured nails. 'All about the new variety you want to try out.'

She came closer to him, and he tensed as though her proximity made him uneasy. Unceremoniously, he thrust the books into her hand and moved to the fire, his back to the leaping flames. His voice was harsh as he said, 'Look at the books later, I'll open the wine now.'

Tara lifted an eyebrow in surprise. What had happened to the warm friendliness? His swift mood changes were bewildering. The paused lengthened uncomfortably, Ben moodily staring at the bottle on the table.

Eventually she shrugged, turning to a small wall cupboard for glasses and a corkscrew.

'Bring the glasses into the kitchen when you're ready. I've a chicken casserole in the oven — there's easily enough for two.'

Later, in the sitting room after they had eaten, Ben seemed more relaxed. 'You're quite a cook!' he complimented her. 'That was no ordinary casserole!' He sighed contentedly and looked around, echoing his earlier comment. 'It feels safe here.'

'Safe,' Tara repeated wonderingly. 'From what? The world? The pressures? People?' She looked at him consideringly and decided to ask, openly, the questions which were nagging her. 'Where are you from, Ben. Why did you stop here, in this sleepy little place? Are you running away from something?'

For a long time he ignored her. The silence continued until Tara began to regret her show of curiosity. She was on the point of apologising for her bad manners when he raised his dark eyes and looked directly at her, one searching look that frightened her.

Then, staring once more into the flames, he said roughly, 'Whatever I was, wherever I was, it's in the past.

And the past is finished with. It's of no importance. I'm here now, that's all I need to tell you — and all that matters.'

Changing swiftly from defence to attack, he asked, 'And what about you? That ultra-glamorous girl on the motorway — there's been little sign of her since last night — I'm glad to say.'

Tara broke in, angrily. 'And if there were? Would you feel obliged to behave in the same boorish way?'

'Can't you forget that? I've said I'm sorry and I meant it. Tell me, instead, about the vineyard owner. What's a beautiful girl like her doing on her own in this backwater?'

In spite of herself, Tara laughed. 'You'll have to do better than that old line.'

Ben laughed with her, and then sobered again. 'All right then. Is there someone special in your life? Have you ever been married, Tara?'

Thrown by his directness, she rushed into speech, saying emphatically, too emphatically, 'Of course not. Marriage is not, and never will be, part of my life.'

Ben's gaze was sceptical, and Tara bit her lip, wishing belatedly she had not been so vehement in her denial.

There was no immediate reply but, after reaching for the bottle and pouring the last of the wine into their empty glasses, he said drily, 'Methinks the lady doth protest too much.' His face was unexpectedly kind, as he looked into her eyes.

'Could it be that you're carrying a torch for anyone, Tara? You've been hurt, haven't you?'

His manner was sympathetic and, to her own surprise, Tara started to tell him about Hugh.

Beguiled by the firelight, the wine, and, most of all, by the persuasive and magnetic presence of the man opposite her, she began. 'It seems a long time ago since . . . '

'Tell me,' Ben murmured, leaning towards her, as her voice tailed away.

'There's not much to tell. It's over

now. I fell in love. I thought he loved me. I thought he wanted total commitment.'

Tara paused; it still pained to talk about it, she discovered and added hurriedly, 'Classic story — when I found out he was married, with a wife and family — I finished it. That's all there is. Satisfied now?'

Ben was still leaning forward but the compassion had gone from his eyes. Instead something glowed there that made her feel uneasy, a strange mixture of anger and excitement. He was like a tautly coiled spring.

When he spoke, it was so softly and so deliberately, she could barely catch what he said. 'And you really didn't know he was married. I can't believe that.'

A flood of unaccustomed self-pity washed over Tara. That she should finally confess her story to someone, after keeping silent so long, and not be believed, was a cruel irony.

She got up edgily; the mood was

definitely broken. 'It's of no importance to me what you believe, but I'm telling the truth,' she snapped angrily.

Then in a neutral voice she said, 'Are you married?'

A change came over his face — a shutter came down.

Eventually, he stated, 'I was — once,' and his eyes dared her to ask any more.

To avoid his brooding look, Tara went to the cassette player and slipped in a tape. For the first time since he had arrived, she felt a frisson of fear. Had she been foolish to invite this volatile, moody stranger into her house? She knew virtually nothing about him, she was alone in the cottage, totally vulnerable, the nearest house half a mile down the lane, and the village almost a mile away.

Berating herself for letting her imagination run away with her, she looked down at him, his eyes were closed, and she noticed how exhausted and tired he looked.

Quietly she slipped into a chair, her

eyes never leaving the face opposite, seeing, once again the face of the buccaneer, the adventurer, now with shadows from the fire chasing across the strong lines of jaw and chin. Cruelty was latent in the deeply sensual mouth, and yet, Tara sensed that he could be capable of great tenderness — and passion too.

Hardly daring to breath she picked up a pencil and paper and began to draw. Totally absorbed in the task of trying to catch the elusive spirit of the man in the chair she worked swiftly and competently.

He woke as suddenly as he had fallen asleep. Glancing up from her paper, she started guiltily, as she met a direct piercing stare.

'What are you doing?'

'Nothing. Just scribbling some notes for tomorrow.' She crumpled the paper and pushed it down hard among the logs in the basket by her chair.

'Let me see.'

The request was innocent but the

tone was deadly, and Tara felt a thrill of excitement mixed with fear.

'I've told you. It's nothing. It's getting late. Would you like some more coffee before you go?'

'I'm not leaving until you show me what's on that paper.'

Tara had half risen from her chair, but he moved swiftly towards her and bent down to retrieve the paper. She moved to stop him, grasping his arm to fend him away from the basket. Ben took hold of her shoulders but she slipped and fell against the chair, pulling him down. For a second or two they grappled for balance, then Tara felt herself steadied, set on her feet and held, loosely at first, then with increasing pressure.

Ben drew her towards him, dark head bending close.

'Tara?' His voice was questioning and hoarse, as his hands slid down to her waist, gathering her closer so that she could feel the hard tension in his body. His mouth, seeking response, found hers.

Tara knew that soon she would be totally lost, unable to withstand him and with all her strength she pushed violently against him.

'No. Don't. Ben, please.'

He was suddenly perfectly still and Tara sensed an immense effort of control. He let her go but as his dark, devouring gaze swept down over her, she thought for a second that he was going to reach for her again.

Instead, he moved back and said softly, 'You're right. I'd better go. Thanks for the supper.' One backward glance and he was gone, the door closing quietly behind him.

For many moments Tara was still, calming her breathing and chaotic thoughts, shaken by the feelings Ben Lavalle had aroused in her.

Then, refusing to dwell any longer on the treacherous reactions of her body, she reached for the crumpled paper in the log basket. Smoothing it out, she studied it for a second, then hurried towards the back stairs that led to her studio.

Tara began sketching out her idea for the portrait when the image was still fresh in her mind, her mind too busy to consider the possibility of a lonely figure standing beneath her window — with longing in his eyes.

Some time later, when the Saab was quietly driven away, Tara did not even hear the sound of the engine.

It was well into the early hours of the morning before the light in the studio went out and Tara, exhausted, dropped into bed.

3

A week later, Ben Lavalle had become an integral part of Tamary Vineyard. He seemed to be a natural leader for the others, even Tom, to turn to for a decision. It was maddening but Tara accepted it because she needed time to work on the portrait. She was feeling increasingly excited about it. She was sure it was going to be the best thing she had ever done, and she was on a tightrope of uncertainty about her opportunity to complete it. If something happened to stop her, and Ben left as abruptly as he had appeared she knew that it would be one of the biggest disappointments of her life.

Tara had always encouraged her workers to come into the cottage for a break during the day and, latterly, this had included Ben. He seldom took a great deal of notice of her if she were present and, indeed, he contributed little to the general camaraderie. When he did speak, however, his deep voice and air of command had a way of silencing the others. Tara concluded that he must be used to being in authority — and also that he preferred, or was more comfortable with the presence of men than women.

He had taken to dropping in frequently, although no mention was ever made of the passionate way they had parted company on that first evening at the cottage. As she become more used to his presence, an uneasy feeling of intimacy had grown up between them. Neither spoke of it during the daylight hours, it was their shared secret. No-one, before him, had attempted to disturb her evening peace. No-one would have been allowed to.

Unacknowledged came the thought that Ben Lavalle, brooding, secretive Ben, had disturbed her peace in more ways than one. She told herself she allowed the intrusion because of her

43

need to study him, but it was doubtful if that was the only reason. Irritating, arrogant, presumptious — he could be all those. Yet, when he looked at her in a certain way, it was electric.

Perhaps the way he treated her in the daytime had piqued her, but she was also curious about him. There was a ruthless core within him and she could not begin to imagine his reaction if he knew she was painting him. She hoped he would never find out.

Seeing his dark head and tall figure not far away, she filled a big flask with coffee, put mugs on a tray, and went out into the fields. She had made a number of sketches from different angles but there never seemed sufficient opportunities to study his buccaneer's face in all its variety of expression. It was frustrating that she had to be so furtive about it.

He was hoeing the earth between neat rows of vines. Putting the tray down she called, 'Ben, coffee.'

He looked up unsmilingly, laid down

the hoe and came over to where she knelt. 'This is a ridiculously labour intensive way to keep the weeds down,' he grumbled as he sprawled on the earth beside her. 'You should instal some automation here. It could double your profits in one year.'

Tara, watching him over the rim of her coffee mug, was memorising the angles of his face and had hardly heard a word he said. She started guiltily as he repeated questioningly 'Tara?'

'Sorry. What did you say?'

'What's the matter with you?' He sounded impatient. 'You don't seem interested in discussions about improving the efficiency of the vineyard. It's your livelihood, you really should be more businesslike — and more open to suggestion.'

Stung by his criticism, Tara was instinctively defensive. She loved her vines, but only as part of the setting for her tranquil life in this serene backwater. Unable to admit that the vineyard, far from being her livelihood, was no more than a pleasurable hobby, she said icily, 'How I choose to run my business is hardly a subject for discussion with a casual labourer.'

This crushing retort failed signally to have the effect she had hoped. Ben only raised an eyebrow and gave a dry laugh. 'If that ill-mannered comment is meant to put me in my place, it's not going to work, I'm afraid. You may have noticed that I'm not the cap doffing type — least of all to a woman!' Before Tara could gather her resources to object to this chauvinistic remark, he went on. 'Also, I'm curious about why you're so against the thought of mechanisation. Since I'm such a thorn in your flesh you must realise that you wouldn't need people like me if you used, for instance, spray weedkillers.'

'Good grief. I've been determined, from the beginning, to do nothing of the sort. My methods are totally organic — and they're going to remain so. I shouldn't have to, and won't, explain my reasons for that choice to you — or anyone.'

Tara's answer was short, but her irritation was growing. All she had come for was a discreet chance to observe him, before returning to her studio. Instead, she was finding herself involved in a probing which could, if not deflected, require the sort of explanations she did not want to give. If her secret was exposed and the media discovered where Tamara lived, the harassment to the villagers could be deeply embarrassing. All her carefully nurtured relationship with the local people would change overnight if it became known that she was a celebrity.

Ben, looking hard at her and watching her frown, had clearly gained the wrong idea. When he spoke again, he seemed more hesitant than usual, picking his words carefully. 'If it's money you need, initially, to change things, I could help. It would be no problem — a proper financial footing, of course. Maybe a partnership?'

Tara was speechless. How dare he? It

was an intrusion of the worst kind. How dare he come along, accept a menial job, and display such arrogance with his condescending dislike of women? She said violently, 'No, I don't want that. I don't need it. There's absolutely no question of it.'

Then, gathering her forces for a counter attack she added sarcastically, 'How is it you're such an expert? Have you ever worked in a vineyard before — or even run a business?'

Being certain that he, also, wanted to preserve the secret of his background, she saw that she had touched him on the raw. A muscle in his face twitched and she saw, with unexpected contrition, that he flinched. He was instantly in control of himself again, so that she wondered if she had imagined that vulnerable look. His voice was steady as he answered, without apparent heat, 'As it happens, I have both worked in a vineyard and run a business.'

Tara, conscious that she has got him to divulge something about his past, said, encouragingly, 'Tell me about it.'

Once again, she saw dislike in his face. She was not used to being looked at like that. In one lithe, catlike movement, he got to his feet, forcing her to look up to him. 'No, I don't think I will.' As he spoke he picked up the hoe. 'You'd better take that coffee on to your next port of call — unless you really want to look at me some more.'

Choking back a retort, Tara walked away with a heightened colour. It was maddening that he had noticed her looking at him and was aware of the closeness with which she studied him. But it was even more insufferable that he had interpreted it as a different kind of interest. Calming her anger with an effort, she continued into the next field, speculating on the past of the man she had just left. So, he had worked in a vineyard, had he? And owned a business. The mention of them had certainly got under his skin.

She took the empty mugs back to the

cottage. Tom and she had arranged to meet at the pub for lunch. Since most of her dealings with her young manager were carried out in this informal way she thought nothing of it — until she arrived at The Black Swan and found, not just Tom, but Ben Lavalle as well. The two of them were already deep in conversation. With dismay she knew as soon as Tom got up, asking her, a little too heartily, what she would like to drink, that they had been talking about the vineyard.

It isn't fair, Tara thought rebelliously. Ben has been getting at Tom as well. Now he'll be probing, too. As she accepted a drink and settled down at the table in the dark corner of the ancient pub she was mentally preparing, ready for the inevitable conflict. The smile she gave Ben was wary but he met it with an amused, completely comprehending one. One of his most dangerous characteristics was that he always seemed to know what she was thinking or what mood she was in. With something to hide, this was disconcerting.

While Tom was out of earshot at the bar counter, Ben said softly, intimately, 'May I come tonight?' His eyes caught and held her gaze and his hand came out and covered hers but she pulled it away in a gesture that she instantly regretted, recognising it for being childishly pettish.

'I suppose so.' Her voice, too, she thought ashamedly, sounded cross, and she tried to make amends by putting her feelings into words. 'But, after this morning — in the fields — perhaps it's not such a good idea.' Even as she spoke, it occurred to her that to keep him away was to risk losing her best opportunity of continuing with the portrait.

Tom was back, standing beside them, carrying a tin tray. Putting it down on the dark wooden table, he eased into the settle beside Tara. 'Thanks, Tom. Cheers.' She lifted her glass and the others did likewise. Then, as though on cue, both Ben and Tom put their elbows on the table and said, with emphasis, 'Now, about the vineyard.'

They both laughed and sat back, offering the other the first chance to speak, but before either could continue, Tara, feeling even more conspired against, intervened, saying coldly, 'Tom, if there's anything to discuss, I would prefer it to be private.'

She looked daggers at Ben but it was Tom that the remark affected. 'Actually, Tara, it's Ben's ideas that I wanted to talk to you about — they really do make good sense.' He saw her gather breath for a retort and hurried on, 'But it's not just from Ben — lots of his proposed innovations are things I've wanted to do for ages — they'd improve efficiency and the product. I'd like to show you a few figures.'

He took the paper from his jacket pocket but Tara held up a dismissive hand. 'I'm sorry, Tom, but no. Definitely not. There are no figures that I want to see because nothing is going to be changed. Not now. Not ever. Your friend, Mr Lavalle, should have told you that.'

The derogatory way she spoke was acid, even to her own ears, and she was inwardly ashamed. Particularly as Tom, the paper still in his hand, was looking crushed. But she had to nip these dangerous suggestions in the bud. So she hardened her heart. 'I have no interest whatsoever in changing my vineyard into a large prosperous concern. I like it exactly as it is. I like selling to local restaurants. I like producing organic wine. That's final!'

She lifted her glass, drained it, and slapped it down decisively. Two pairs of eyes were staring at her; one blue pair hurt and puzzled, one grey pair, cold, hard, and equally puzzled. Defensively, Tara said to Tom, 'I thought you liked things the way they are. You seemed happy enough with everything — before Mr Lavalle descended on us.' Then, switching her attack to Ben, she said scathingly,

'Why did you have to come and interfere?'

'Tara.' Tom spoke her name reproachfully. His look at Ben, was one of conciliation and it fuelled Tara's wrath even further to know that he was mutely apologising on her behalf. Haltingly, he went on, 'It just isn't like you to be so sarcastic to anyone — or so rude.'

'Isn't it? Then, perhaps it's time I changed. It's *my* vineyard — *my* business. Doesn't that stand for anything?' Her voice had grown unconsciously louder and she saw one or two heads turn to look at her.

'Hardly a democratic attitude, is it?' Ben's voice, by contrast, was low and unemotional. She tried to ignore him but Ben Lavalle was not an easy person to ignore or intimidate. He said questioningly, 'Aren't you interested in the needs of your employees? And are you too proud, too sophisticated, to join them? I've never seen you do a full day's work in the vineyard. It seems to me that you're just playing at it.'

Poor Tom was looking uncomfortable but Ben's face showed, not just awareness of the fact that he was putting her on the spot, but also bafflement. Tom, caught in the current of electric animosity between them said, 'She has her own work to do, don't you Tara? In London.'

It sounded ridiculously vague and Tara, making a sudden decision, said to Tom, 'If it's money, I'll raise your wages. I'd already thought about that.'

He muttered, 'Thanks. But that wasn't what it was all about,' and fell silent.

Ben's look at her was hard and searching. His eyes narrowed as he leaned towards her. 'You're an enigma, Tara. I don't understand you. If it's not profit; if you don't need the vineyard, what is it you have to hide? Why the huge window in the roof? What goes on in your cottage? Have you got a mad woman locked away? Somebody's wife, perhaps?' His tone was full of meaning.

55

'Who puts up all the money — or can I guess?'

Tara gasped in outrage. Dimly she was aware of Tom's horrified 'Here, steady on,' but she did not wait for him to defend her from Ben's attack. Getting angrily to her feet, she shouted furiously, 'Since none of this is your business — you're fired! Pay anything to Mr Lavalle that we owe him, please, Tom. I'm not staying here any longer.' Then, pushing impetuously by, she was gone, heartily thankful to be away from the inquisition and back in the fresh air. She took several deep breaths; the pub had been claustrophobic, but she knew she had acquitted herself badly.

As she strode back to the cottage, long, blue jeaned legs flashing, she wished that she had been cooler, parried the questions lightly, instead of exploding into anger. It had been so awkward for Tom but Ben Lavalle was impossible, especially when he had leaped to the wrong conclusion. He obviously believed that she had a sugar daddy in the background — she, the most independent of women. But how was she ever going to finish the portrait now?

By evening, Tara, who had shut herself in the studio and worked solidly for five hours, was physically tired but emotionally calmed. Painting had ever been her best therapy and the portrait could, she believed, now be finished from memory. It was regrettable but it could be done. Ben Lavalle had been like a hurricane in her life, too disturbing, too upsetting, too exciting. She had cut him out of it now, just as she had once cut Hugh out, and she would be all the better for the loss.

With the fire lit, she put a tape in the cassette and snuggled into a chair with a glass in her hand, trying to recapture the peaceful mood of her evenings. Somehow it didn't work, there was something missing. Nevertheless, restless as she was, the doorbell made her jump. Surely it couldn't be Ben — not after what had happened?

Her heart beat quicker and she opened the door — and stood still in amazement. 'Hugh,' she cried, 'I can't believe it. What on earth are you doing here?'

The tall, fair man smiled widely, showing even white teeth under a luxuriant blond moustache. He held out both hands in a gesture familiar to Tara but which she saw now was a trifle theatrical. Pointedly, she stood back, refusing the proffered embrace.

'What am I doing here, Tara? Surely you don't have to ask, darling. I've missed you too much. I couldn't stay away any longer.'

Tara looked at him. His mouth curled up at the corners as he said easily, caressingly, 'Aren't you going to ask me in? Do we have to talk on the doorstep?

How confident he was, how sure that she had missed him and would have him back. As she stepped aside to allow him to pass she said, 'There isn't anything to talk about, Hugh. It was all over long ago. You were married and you didn't have the decency to tell me. It's finished. You can come in and have a drink since you're here, but that's all.'

Appearing undaunted by her refusal to turn back the clock, he came into the cottage, dropping a light kiss on her brow as he went past. 'It isn't finished between us, Tara love. How could it be? I've thought about you every day since you cruelly booted me out of your life.'

'I'm sorry, Hugh, but I haven't thought about you.' It sounded abrasive, but, after all, he had decieved and hurt her. Also, as she said it, Tara realised that it was true. She hadn't thought about him for a long time. The wound had faded into nothing more than a faint scar. And now, as she watched him stretch out on the couch and pat the edge invitingly, she was seeing him with eyes that were totally unblinkered.

His smile faded and he sounded like a sulky boy as he said, 'Don't be ridiculous. We were everything to each other.'

'Everything?' Tara's laugh was hollow. 'Correction, Hugh. You were everything to me — or I thought you were. But you had a secret — a home life — a wife and a child.'

A thought came unbidden. There was another man with a secret. Was it possible that his mysterious background included a wife and child, too?'

Hugh lit a cigarette and said wheedlingly, 'I admit I was wrong to lie. But haven't I paid long enough for that? Isn't it time my sentence was over?'

Tara was on the point of a vehement refusal when she heard a knocking on the back door. Quickly she went to answer it. Framed in the doorway was what seemed to be a large bouquet of flowers with legs. From behind it, came the familiar deep voice. 'These are in the nature of an apology. I'm holding them in front of me for protection. Is it safe to come out?' He lowered the flowers and showed her a smiling face that, yet, held a hint of anxiety. More seriously, he said, 'I'm truly sorry, Tara. Tom took me to task very severely. I had no right to say — to assume — the things I did. Will you forgive me?'

'Yes, of course. I behaved badly, too.' She was acutely conscious of the presence in the sitting-room behind her. Leaning forward she almost snatched the flowers, saying breathlessly, 'They're beautiful. I'll put them in water. But if you don't mind, Ben, I won't ask you in tonight. I'm awfully tired and ... ' Her voice trailed off as Hugh came lounging up behind her. Glass in one hand, cigarette in the other, he had removed his tie and jacket, appearing very much at ease.

'Surely you're not going to send the poor man away, love? After bringing you half of Kew Gardens, too?' His voice was silky but there was a dangerous glint in his eyes.

Ben's smile had faded as he looked from one to the other. Over his face crept a look of dawning comprehension. 'I see,' he said slowly.

'This is Hugh,' Tara interrupted. 'He's an old friend. You remember I told you about him.' She knew she sounded evasive. Why, oh why, had Hugh chosen this night of all others to appear? She rushed on. 'It was such a surprise, having him turn up unexpectedly.' Feeling Hugh's arm descend proprietorally across her shoulders, she wanted to cry out that she hadn't asked him and didn't want him.

Ben's expression had become contemptuous, as though all his suspicions had been confirmed. Sarcastically he said, 'Since your old friend has turned up — and so unexpectedly — I wouldn't dream of intruding. Goodnight, Tara.' And was gone.

She flung herself from Hugh's grasp. From the safety of the other side of the kitchen she glared at him. 'You behaved abominably. You know perfectly well that you made him think we were lovers — and you did it on purpose.'

'Is that so bad?' Hugh was deliberately provocative. 'What is he to you, anyway. Do I have cause to be jealous?'

'No, Hugh.' Tara spoke evenly and calmly. Now was the time to convince him, once and for all, that they were finished. 'You have neither cause nor right to be anything at all as far as I am concerned. I told you before to get out of my life. I meant it then and mean it now.' Going into the living-room she picked up his jacket and held it out to him, avoiding his attempt to grab her as he took it.

'You mean it, don't you?' He sounded incredulous as he shrugged on his coat. His face had assumed an ugly look.

'Yes, I mean it. You've finally got the message.' Tara was weary of this. What had she ever seen in this conceited man to make her believe herself in love with him? Holding open the door she could not avoid his embrace this time, but she kept completely still, reacting not at all to his kisses and greedy hands.

After a moment he raised his head and looked into her expressionless face, as though he could not believe she was not aroused by him. 'OK. If that's the way it is — fine!' he muttered. 'I wish you joy of your country bumpkin.'

Tara knew better than to jump to Ben's defence. She must do nothing to stop Hugh leaving — that was all that mattered.

When the sound of his car had died away she began arranging flowers into vases, her mind as busy as her hands. How could she convince Ben that his version of the scene he had witnessed was incorrect? She was not Hugh's mistress: she was not a kept woman and never had been. Somehow it was imperative to her peace of mind that Ben should know the truth. But how could she reach him — and would he believe her?

An hour later he rang.

As soon as she recognised his voice Tara rushed into speech. 'It wasn't what you think. I hadn't seen him for ages and I'd no idea that he would drop in.' Then hearing her own pleading tone she regained her natural spirit and added. 'Although why I should bother to explain to you, I don't know.'

'Neither do I.' His voice was cold. 'Is he there now?'

'No. I told him to leave — for ever — about two minutes after you'd gone.'

'Did you indeed?' There was a silence on the end of the line, then he said, with more warmth, 'I came tonight because I'd decided it was time to show you something. Something that will help you to understand my interest in the vineyard — and — other things. Can you pack a case and be ready to leave tomorrow morning? I've got air tickets to Lyons, and there'll be a car waiting there. We'll be away about three days.'

'What?' Tara could hardly believe her ears. 'You're asking me to go away with you for a . . . for a . . . ?

'Dirty week-end?' His laugh was genuine. 'No, of course not. There's somewhere in France I want you to see. So, be ready at ten. Good-night.'

And without even waiting for her amazed 'Good-night', he rang off, leaving her bemused, curious, a little resentful at such high-handed assumptions but, above all, excited. Oh yes, she would go all right. But what on earth was it that he wanted to show her?

4

Tara stared at the phone for a long time after Ben had rung off, wondering why she'd agreed so readily to go away with him. He hadn't explained a thing. His confident arrogance was overwhelming, especially since she'd sacked him only that morning — a small thing that both of them appeared to have forgotten. Now she seemed to be acting Trilby to his Svengali! It was ridiculous!

Three days away with Ben Lavalle! Three days away from the portrait — but at least she'd have the opportunity to study her subject. Whatever doubts she had about the coming trip, she was committed.

Fired with excitement, and piqued by curiosity, she found it hard to sleep. Ben's face dominated her brain, teasing her spirit with its dark ambiguity, and challenging her technical skill with its elusive expression. Bitter past experiences lay in the shadows of his eyes, which also expressed a deep, dark pessimism about the future.

Tara squeezed her lids tightly together, but the vision loomed larger and larger. It was no good. With an exasperated sigh, she switched on the light, got up, pulled on sweater and jeans, and went up to the studio.

★　★　★

'You look tired!' Ben's unflattering comment met her on the cottage doorstep promptly at ten o'clock the next morning. He frowned. 'Hectic night from the look of it. Hugh came back later, did he?'

'No, he did not. I told you, it's over. I was . . . ' Tara stopped in time. She couldn't admit to working on his portrait until nearly dawn. 'I didn't sleep much,' she lamely trailed off.

'I hope you're ready, we've a plane to catch.'

Tara peered at him more closely. It was hard to see behind the glasses whether she'd really captured the expression which so intrigued her.

'Tara, come on. Stop staring at me like that. Where's your case?'

Disappointed, she opened the door wider to let him in. 'I didn't actually agree to come. It's not so easy to take three days off — just like that.'

'I hardly think your business will fold, just because you're away for a day or two. Tom seems to have things very much under control.'

The sarcastic edge to his voice annoyed her, with its implication that she didn't have control, and for a moment she seriously considered slamming the door on him. But her curiosity was too acute, and the thought wouldn't go away that three days with Ben Lavalle could be interesting. Maybe some of the questions surrounding him would be answered. She might even find out something about him.

She did! He was well organised, and

a very fast, but expert, driver! The Saab made the journey from Tamary Hollow to Heathrow in well under three hours. Ben hardly spoke, and refused to answer Tara's questions about where they were heading — or why!

'Just sit back and enjoy the journey. Don't you like surprises, Tara?' He took his eyes off the motorway for the briefest of glances at her.

'Not particularly,' she lied, still unfairly blaming him for her sleepless night.

He laughed, and put his left hand on her arm — a firm, warm touch. 'Don't be such a spoilsport. You're obviously in a bad mood this morning. Whatever's bothering you — just forget it for the next three days. I'll take care of things. Try and have a sleep now. You look as though you need it.'

'Thanks.' Tara's intended sarcasm was affected by a sudden jaw-cracking yawn, and her natural good humour reasserted itself. After all, he was right, she did need some sleep, and it was an unexpectedly pleasurable sensation to let someone else take charge of things for a change. She only hoped he'd never guess what was bothering her.

'OK, you win,' she conceded, 'wake me up when we get there.'

'Good girl.' His approving pat on the arm and 'father to child' tone didn't please her at all, but she closed her eyes and instantly fell asleep.

Ben woke her up to board the plane. She recalled little of the journey except a vague remembrance of a plastic airline lunch, then a swift transition to hire car, and a powerful surge of speed, this time heading southwards on the French autoroute. She had always been able to cat-nap, any place, any time — a habit acquired from her erratic working schedule, when she worked through the night, seeing no point in blocking her inspirational flow just because it was the conventional bed-time. It was a measure of her subconscious trust in Ben Lavalle's capability, that she slept soundly through most of the journey.

His deep voice drifted into her dreams. 'Tara, wake up, we're nearly there.' He sounded amused. 'You have a most enviable talent of being able to sleep through anything.'

She struggled into a more upright position, blinked, and ran her hands through her long hair, massaging her scalp. Judging by the shadows outside, it was late afternoon. They were off the autoroute, and well into the French countryside. 'Where . . . ?'

'You'll see,' he interrupted. 'Feeling better?'

'Much. Ben, please, do tell me where we are, and where we're going.'

'What a mercy you've been asleep. Until now, at least, I haven't been plagued by questions,' he said good humouredly. 'We're about a hundred miles south of Lyon, on the western side of the River Rhona, and this . . . ' unexpectedly, he swung the car off the road, and through a high gateway, ' . . . is what I've brought you to see.' He reduced speed to drive up a wide-gravelled track and Tara saw, stretching away on both sides of the road, vines in young green leaf, gently undulating away in the distance.

'A vineyard,' she gasped.

'Brilliant! An amazing piece of deduction.' He turned to her and her nerve ends zinged as his dark eyes smiled directly into hers. He looked years younger, a high excitement animating his usually closed expression.

'But, why . . . ?' Tara didn't quite know what she felt. She was still trying to calm that electric tingle that had surged through her when Ben had smiled at her. It had been a glimpse of a man unfettered by his past. A man happy to be in the present.

He put his finger to his lips. 'Shh . . . wait and see.'

The driveway ended at a mass of stone buildings, dominated by a gracious four storeyed house with shuttered windows and low tiled roof. There had been a sign over the arched entry, but Tara had only caught the words

73

'Domaine' and 'Caves'. She realised that they were in a sizeable vineyard, probably with commercial tastings to the public. A coach stood in the courtyard, revving up to pull away, and she saw two young women, one talking to the driver, the other helping an elderly passenger onto the bus, which moved off as Ben drove up to the steps of the house.

'Just a moment.' He turned to Tara. 'Wait here, I'll see if they're ready for us.' He got out of the car, slamming the door.

Glad of a second's respite, Tara ran a brush through her hair, took a quick look at her face, and decided that only a full repair job would put it right. The small pocket mirror didn't do justice to her green eyes, which shone with soft awareness of something she hadn't yet acknowledged. Her gaze followed Ben's tall figure as he spoke to the two women. They seemed excited, laughing and talking, one of them holding on tightly to his arm. The smaller girl, dark haired and pretty, reached up to kiss him on the cheek, and Tara felt a stab of jealousy. He must know these girls well; he was very much at ease with them.

He turned back to the car, and opened the passenger door. 'It's all right. You can have a quick look round now, and a more leisurely tour tomorrow. This is Lucy . . . ' he indicated the petite one, ' . . . and this is Jayne.' She was taller, more statuesque — a blue-eyed blonde. 'They'll show you round. This is Tara Cresswell — from Devon. She has a small vineyard there, and I thought she'd be interested in seeing what's been done here.'

So, this was Ben's surprise! For a moment anger welled up. He was still trying to get his own way, to make her change, run her vineyard differently. She turned on him and hissed, 'You've got a nerve, Ben Lavalle. I've told you. I'm not interested in your ideas. It's too . . . '

He moved forward and gripped her forearms. She felt a searing heat where his fingers dug into her flesh. His face was close to hers. 'Listen, and look, Tara. Don't be so difficult. I'm not asking you to change, if you don't want to. I presumed you'd be interested. It is your livelihood — wine making, isn't it? His eyes held hers, and Tara saw with dismay, the lurking contempt there. 'Unless, of course, you've got a private income.'

So, he hadn't believed her story about Hugh, and still thought she was financially dependent on him. She turned away. Trying to convince him would be hopeless. 'All right,' she sighed, 'I would like to look round.'

Jayne and Lucy had stood by, looking anxious and faintly embarrassed at their exchange, but Lucy stepped forward now with hand outstretched. 'Welcome, Tara. We're pleased you could come. Ben, if you'll bring the cases into the house, we'll have tea, and then take Tara round the vines. We've got bikes, if you'd prefer to cycle. It won't be dark for a while yet.'

'I'd love that.' Tara's spirits began to lift. After all, it would be interesting to look around a big vineyard. Tamary Vineyard was very small fry compared to this. 'Shouldn't we take our luggage to the hotel?' she asked Ben, sure that he would have made the necessary arrangements.

'Hotel? I haven't booked a hotel. There's no need.'

'But, where . . . ?' She shook her head in bewilderment.

Jayne said, 'You're staying here, of course. Wasn't that the idea, Ben?'

'It's a hotel — as well as a winery?' Tara looked around in pleasure. It was a lovely spot, quiet now in the evening sun.

'No, it's not a hotel,' Lucy corrected. 'I don't think we could cope with that, as well as all the things we've had to do here.'

'Didn't you notice the crest at the entrance?' Jayne took Tara's overnight bag from Ben, and led the way into the house.

'No. I was still a bit sleepy.'

It was Jayne who pointed out the maroon and gold painted signboard on the wall of one of the stone buildings adjoining the house. 'In there we show videos of our wine-making techniques — part of the guided tour. That side of the business is developing well. You were right, Ben, as usual.' She smiled at him as he put an arm affectionately across her shoulders.

'Thanks to you and Lucy that it's going so well. I'm glad something is.'

Tara was standing open-mouthed at the dominating signboard. 'But I don't understand. Why didn't you say. Is there a connection?'

'Of course.' They had reached the front door of the old house. 'Like the sign says — 'Domaine de Lavalle'. It belongs to . . . '

' . . . Our family,' Ben cut in quickly. 'Lucy and Jayne are my sisters. They're responsible for the day to day running of the vineyard.'

'Why didn't you tell me?' Tara cried.

'Don't you think it was unfair to pretend you were a casual labourer at Tamary Hollow?' She felt a fool, recalling how dismissive she'd been of Ben's suggestions. He'd misled and deceived her.

He shrugged. 'I am a casual labourer at Tamary Hollow. And I never pretended otherwise.'

'How long have you had — all this?' She looked back over the courtyard and the rolling acres of vines beyond.

'Do you think we could go inside, rather than discussing the history of Domaine de Lavalle on the doorstep?' Ben's tone was not entirely friendly. 'If you want to see around before dark, we'd better hurry.' He sensed her resentment, and was defensively cold.

Lucy and Jayne did their best to lighten the tension, and their warm friendliness and obvious pride in the lovely old house melted away Tara's resistance. Especially on the evening cycle ride round the estate.

Ben left them, roaring away in the

Saab on some mysterious errand of his own. 'It's not necessary for me to come. I'll do the technical stuff tomorrow.'

As they cycled through the rows of vines, planted up to both sides of the road, she tried to prise out some information about Ben, but his sisters were evasive, and dribbled out the facts reluctantly, preferring to question her about her own vineyard in Devon.

'Ben told us it's organic — and quite small,' Lucy said. The road was quiet, not much more than a rural track, and the three girls rode side by side.

'Yes, I plan to keep it that way — in spite of Ben.' She tried to change the direction of the conversation. 'So, how long have you owned this?' she asked again.

'We don't own it, it belongs to Ben. He's actually our step-brother, though he's always felt like a real brother to us. Our father's first wife, Jeanne Lavalle, left the vineyard to Ben with a request that he keep the name Lavalle. Our name is Anderson — very British.'

'And your parents — Ben's step-mother?'

'Dad died, and our mother lives in Cheltenham.'

Tara looked surprised. 'So the vineyard's been Ben's for a long time?'

'Yes, but it was pretty run down — until Ben's aunt left him a fortune a year or so back.'

'He was away at the time,' Lucy said chattily, adding proudly, 'so we had to be in charge of the alterations.'

Jayne shot Lucy a warning look. 'We should be getting back now,' she chipped in quickly. 'You've seen the extent of the vineyard — the vines too. We're pleased with them. There should be a good crop this year.'

'You can never be sure though. Anything can happen: the weather, diseases, as you must know, Tara. It's a hard way of making a living, especially on a small scale. That's why we've expanded so much lately. Turn right here. We'll go back through the village. It's really pretty.'

'We were so lucky to be able to expand. Ben's modernised and diversified. It's a sound business now, and the co-operative centre for lots of small local vineyards.'

'So why doesn't he live here, too?' Tara asked.

There was a pause, then Lucy said hastily, 'Jayne and I run it now. We love living in France. I'm getting married next year — Pierre owns a vineyard, too, on the other side of the Rhone.'

'But doesn't Ben want to . . .'

The sisters exchanged looks, and Lucy said firmly, 'We'd better ride in single file — there's the village.'

And that was all Tara learned about Ben Lavalle.

Lucy's Pierre came to supper, bringing an extraordinarily good looking man called Phillippe, who appeared to be besotted with Jayne's cool, blonde English looks. The food and wine — from Domaine de Lavalle, of course — were excellent, and Tara felt herself relaxing in the enjoyment of the lively meal. At the opposite end of the table, Ben's dark face was animated and expressive. The talk was mostly geared to wine, past vintages, future hopes, modernisation techniques, or markets. It was all a bit over Tara's head, and she felt somewhat of a fraud as they tried to draw her into their discussions.

'Honestly,' she protested, after Pierre had asked her if her vines in Devon were prone to eel worm and meal moth, 'I don't know a lot about it yet. I have a manager, and it's a tiny operation compared with yours.'

'Tara's a bit of a wine dilettante,' Ben cut in. 'Profit seems to be at the bottom of her priority list. Nice position to be in,' he added laconically. 'I'm hoping to show her how we do things here tomorrow. Tom, her vineyard manager, at least, is keen to modernise.'

'Perhaps you should have brought him,' Tara shot back.

Ben looked at her, his dark eyes scrutinising her intently. 'Perhaps I should. I never thought of it,' he said levelly.

Tara's heart sank. It was impossible to explain that the vineyard was just a hobby, and that she didn't need the money. As long as it could support the workers, and break even, she didn't care.

'Anyway,' she said, rather desperately, 'this is France — the Rhone — a great wine producing area. Tamary Hollow's Devon — England. There's the world of difference between the two.'

'Absolutely,' Pierre said, gazing adoringly at Lucy, and switching to his main pre-occupation. 'When are you going to name the day? I can't wait much longer for you.'

Lucy returned his look with eyes full of love, and Tara felt inexplicably lonely. The two couples were so obviously in love, she and Ben were the outsiders — jagged edges tacked onto the perfect square.

★ ★ ★

The next day, Ben took her through the Lavalle wine-making process, from grape varieties to the finished bottled product. It was a slick, efficient operation, and Tara was impressed, not only by his knowledge of vines and wines, but at his business acumen and enthusiasm. They ended up in the tasting 'cave', not the main one used for tourist visitors, but a private one in the cellar, housing the vats of wine quietly maturing in their huge casks. It was dark and cool, a pleasant change from the heat of the day outside.

'It's like a cathedral,' Tara whispered.

'A temple to Bachus, if you like.' Ben laughed. 'So, what do you think, Tara? Have you picked up anything useful — for Tamary Hollow?' He took a dusty bottle from a rack. 'Let's try this — it's about ready now.' He polished a couple of glasses, uncorked the bottle, and poured the dark red wine. He held it up to the light. 'Good colour. Taste it,' he commanded.

He was so close to her, she could see

the tiny creases of laughter lines at the corner of his eyes. He'd not laughed a lot since she'd known him. His expression was shuttered now, concentrating on the wine. She longed to touch the lines, to bring softness back to the stern contours of his face — the face that was the subject of her portrait!

'Tara? Aren't you going to try it?'

She blinked, and cast down her eyes. The atmosphere of the dim cellar, just the two of them alone, had beguiled her. She must pull herself together. Ben Lavalle was not a man she could reach. He was too defensive — too hardened. She sighed, sipped, and twirled the taste around her mouth before swallowing. 'It's good,' she pronounced. 'Lots of fruit. But, Ben, you must realise we can't make wine like this at Tamary. It's not far south enough, and . . .'

'Of course, I know that,' Ben broke in impatiently, 'and I'm not suggesting you try. That would be lunatic. But you could improve your methods and make a much better, more saleable, product. I can't understand why you won't even consider it. Don't you want the best? For Tamary? For your workers?'

His look of frustrated bafflement touched Tara's heart. She longed to confide in him, to clear away the misunderstanding. What harm would it do if he did know she was Tamara? Then she remembered the portrait, painted without his knowledge or permission. But was that so very terrible? She couldn't be sure of his reaction. He was volatile, enigmatic. She knew so little about him.

Abruptly she asked, 'Ben, why don't you live here, at Domaine de Lavalle?'

Immediately the dark frown returned. He moved away from her. 'What's that to do with improving your vineyard?'

'Nothing. I'd just like to know something about you. That's all.'

'Before you commit yourself to changing things at Tamary Hollow?' His voice was cold, incredulous. 'If that's all it means to you, I've been wasting my time. You don't need to know anything about me. Your vineyard — my life — they're entirely separate.' He recorked the bottle. 'We'll finish this at supper. The girls will be interested in testing it.'

OK, Tara thought, if that's how you want to play it, you keep your secrets, and I'll keep mine. But the thought brought her little comfort.

They were due to leave next morning. Tara slept badly, and came downstairs late to a breakfast of coffee and croissants in the kitchen. The door was open. She heard her name, and paused outside the door.

Lucy was speaking. ' . . . working for Tara. I wish you'd come back here, Ben.'

'You know I can't — yet. I'm nowhere near finished what I have to do in England. I'm getting there, but there's still a lot to uncover.'

There was a pause, which Tara registered as a gloomy one, and she was about to go in when Jayne said, 'Well, anyway, I like your girlfriend. She's nice.'

There was no pause before the swift answer to that one. 'She's not my girlfriend — and she's already got . . . '

Not wanting to hear any more, Tara went quickly into the kitchen to join the Lavalles for breakfast. She felt it was high time to return to Devon.

5

Securely settled back home into her favourite niche, it was as though she'd never been away. Except that Ben Lavalle now loomed so large in her mind, she was sure nothing would ever be quite the same again! Firmly she put that thought aside.

Everything, Tom assured her, had been ticking over nicely, during their absence. His eyes were assessing — did she imagine that they were also reproachful? Surely not! She was her own woman and Tom knew it. He was, however, far too polite to ask her any direct questions.

At least it was a relief to feel back in control — at the helm of her own ship once more. As the days went by and turned into weeks, Ben's importance, in her mind, gradually diminished as he became more of a shadowy figure. He was settled back into the inn and she only saw him working in the fields in the distance, or in the company of the others when they gathered in her kitchen at coffee time.

Tara was only glad he was still there because she needed to continue studying him for the portait, or so she told herself! She had been working on it in her spare minutes, nonetheless, the fact of his continued presence was nagging at her. She came to the conclusion that it was totally illogical. What possible reason could the owner of a chateau in France have for doing casual, part-time work on someone else's much smaller vineyard. And one, moreover, where he didn't approve of the methods, the scale of the operation or the lack of sophistication. It didn't make sense.

Naturally it crossed her mind that there might be a more personal reason for his presence. But to contemplate that was folly. He gave no sign of having any interest other than his work. Even the evenings at her cottage had ceased.

Mostly she dismissed such speculation and took herself off to her studio. There was much to be done.

Derek was planning the next exhibition and Tara knew she could not neglect the pieces she had promised him would be ready. She worked solidly, producing painting after painting, none of them, she was convinced, of the same quality as the portrait of Ben.

The subject of her best work to date dropped the bombshell during a lunchtime session in the cottage. Both he and Tom were enjoying Tara's home-made soup at the time. She had offered everyone soup and sandwiches on this particular day but the others had either brought their own or were going home for their lunch hour. As Tom said, there wasn't a great deal to do, the crops were coming along nicely and it was a fairly quiet time as they worked up towards harvest.

Ben said lightly, 'I'm glad to hear that, Tom. It means you won't mind my pushing off.'

Tara spilled some hot soup onto her wrist.

'You all right?' Tom was concerned at her sudden exclamation. Ben said nothing but his all-seeing, all-knowing eyes met hers.

Angry with herself for giving away her sharp reaction, she said, a little breathlessly, 'Sorry, it was hot. I was clumsy,' and waited to hear Ben's explanation of when and where he was going. Being Ben, of course he didn't give one, and it was left to Tom to ask when he would be off and for how long.

'Don't know.' Ben was laconic. He added, 'I have to go to London — for business reasons — and it seemed a good time. You'll not need me until the picking now, will you?'

Tom assured him that was fine but Tara was conscious of feeling a growing resentment. He thought he could walk in and out of her life — and her vineyard — to suit himself. His arrogance was incredible!

Consequently, when he lingered,

after Tom had returned to the fields and asked her, fairly offhandedly, if he could take her out to the inn to dinner, as a thank you for the times she had fed him, she was too angry not to off-load some of her grievance.

'No I'm busy.'

Ben's look was remote. He said quietly, 'You don't know which night I was going to suggest.'

Tara, dangerously sparkling said, 'I'm busy every night.'

'I see. That rather puts me in my place doesn't it.'

He turned to go and Tara rushed into speech. Why couldn't he argue with her instead of meekly accepting that she didn't want to see him — when it really wasn't true. 'I'm tired of the way you use this place — and me.'

'Use!' Ben looked astounded, as though he had never heard of the word.

'Yes.' He was looking so baffled that she was forced into further explanation.

'You come and go as you wish. You criticise the way things are run. Now that I know you have your own place, I find it ridiculous. Why do you work here at all? It's obvious you don't need the money. So why?'

Ben's face had adopted a mulish, brooding look. Clearly he was not used to being called to account and did not like it.

He said bitingly, 'That's a lot of 'whys'.' I do what I was employed for. Anything else is my own affair.'

Tara knew that he was right but she was too furious to back off. 'Maybe it is.' She said it violently. 'But I want to know why here? Why my place? Why me?'

He seemed to consider the question. 'I'm not sure.'

But there was an arrested look in his eyes. He gazed steadily at her, as though a new and unwelcome thought had occurred to him.

Tara said sarcastically, 'Actually I know why.'

'You do?' he looked slightly anxious.

'You want to be based somewhere

here in Britain so that you can continue your activities — whatever they are — in London. You're up to something, Ben Lavalle — and I don't want to know what it is. As you say it's none of my business — but I resent your using my place as a jumping off point for whatever you're working on.'

Ben's expression was unfathomable. He said, 'Would it help if I told you there is absolutely nothing criminal or morally wrong about what I am doing? But it's important. I have to do it.'

She was silent and his voice became warmer. 'Look, Tara, I can't explain. Not now. Perhaps never. And yes, it's true that I like being here. It's an idyllic spot and I have a crusading spirit. You know that I'd love to make this place into what it could be.'

She looked up, hotly ready to deny his right to do so, but he placed a finger on her lips. 'No don't say anything. I know how you feel about that. My 'activities' as you call them, are vital to my future. That's as much as I can say.

Will you accept that?'

'I suppose I have to.' Tara was ashamed of her own grudging admission. She waited hopefully for him to re-issue the invitation to dinner. This time she would accept. But Ben, true to form, did not do what was expected of him. He only smiled at her, waved a casual hand in farewell and left.

Yet another unsatisfactory encounter, she thought bitterly. As she cleared up the remains of the meal she crashed crockery down noisily, and turned the tap on far too hard so that water splashed all over the kitchen. He was quite the most irritating man she had ever met. And she would be heartily thankful when he left and peace was restored to Tamary Hollow.

Three days later she had the opportunity to begin enjoying the longed for peace! When Tom came into the cottage on his arrival at work, he told her that Ben had gone. That he'd packed up at the Inn and taken off the night before. So Ben had informed Tom of his departure but had not bothered to tell her. It was so humiliating.

Later in the day Tara found herself snapping waspishly at Tom — and knew why! The humilition was even worse when she realised that Tom did too — or at least guessed!

She tried to make amends by cooking him one of her special omelettes for lunch but even then she was aware that his puppy-dog eyes communicated more than his tongue did. Until Tom said, in his slow country voice, 'Seems to me that you've taken a bit of a shine to Ben. I can't help noticing that there's a sort of chemistry between you. Although you seem to fight a lot.'

The last sentence had a hopeful note about it and Tara was at pains to deny any relationship between herself and Ben Lavalle.

Tom said little more, but two weeks later he brought the subject up again. 'Haven't heard anything from Ben have you Tara?'

'No, of course not, why on earth

should he write to me?'

'Just wondered. Thought he might have mentioned if he'd be coming back.'

'Well he hasn't. And if you still think there was anything between us, surely that's proof enough.'

'I suppose so.' Tom sipped his coffee with an abstracted air, then put the mug on the table. 'Since you tell me so, I believe you. Does that mean there's any hope for me?'

Tara gasped. Had this been under her nose all the time he had been working for her? Suddenly she felt hard done by. Tom was a good manager and she needed him to run the vineyard for her. But complications like this, she could do without.

'Tom, I'm sorry.' She said it awkwardly. 'I'd got no idea you thought of me in that way. I really like you — I thought we were friends but . . .'

Tom smiled. It went a little awry but he managed it. 'So we are.' he said. 'And don't worry, it's all right. I had to ask. It won't make any difference.'

Tara was desperately sorry for him, but giving false hopes was no way to help. She put a hand over his in sympathy. 'We can still be friends can't we, Tom?' she repeated.

His hand turned under hers. He was making a tremendous effort to be the old Tom, the one she had always known before he had let his feelings show. With a visible effort he said gaily, 'Well, Miss Cresswell is it OK to ask a friend to come to the Village Fête with me, next Saturday?'

Tara laughed, relieved to be back on familiar territory. 'I'd love to. In fact I've been making homemade goodies for the cake stall for days.'

Saturday's weather forecast had not been good but the villagers were made of sterner stuff than to give up over storm warnings. The marquee was erected before ten o'clock and all the side stalls were laid out with their offerings. When Tom and Tara arrived, the proceedings had been in full swing for a good half-hour.

At three o'clock the rain began. It didn't start gradually but came down in sheeting torrents at once. There was a flurry of movement as everyone raced for the shelter of the marquee. Tom rushed to help the vicar gather up some of the babies who had been playing happily in a big playpen, and bring them under cover. Within minutes, there was nothing left outside except the deserted trestle tables, rapidly drenched cardboard boxes and forlorn decorations of coloured paper. They watched as the Green became soaked and the lanes turned into flood areas.

It soon became apparent that the marquee itself would not suffice to shelter them for long. The wind began to rise and, as the canvas became weighted down, everyone was in imminent danger of being underneath when it collapsed. Hurried consultations decided everyone to move to the pub or the row of houses next to the Green. The ones with keys made a dash for it first, in order to let everyone else in. Then, carrying children and bags and anything else they wanted to salvage, they ran across the clearing in twos and threes.

From the comparative calm of Mrs Anstey's at No. 6, Tom and Tara watched the ever rising storm with deepening apprehension. Though neither said it to the other they knew that the high wind, which was followed by the heaviest fall of hailstones seen for years, were liable to be wreaking havoc with their vines. And there was nothing they could do. Even going out would be folly while it was raging at this pitch.

There were gasps of horror coming from all around them as, first a chimney was seen to topple, then the inn sign lurched drunkenly sideways as the board was wrenched from its iron frame.

The culmination was the uprooting of an old oak which had withstood many decades of village life. As it wrenched over, and crashed its length onto the Green where all of them had been only half an hour ago, everyone was silent. But that at least appeared to be the signal for the storm to die down. Eventually they all came out, exclaiming and wondering, helping those who needed it and setting to work immediately to start clearing up.

There were roof tiles all over the grass. They had been flying around at the height of the gusts as though they were feathers. Tom urged Tara to go home, and he would join her as soon as he had done what he could for the villagers. But she would have none of it, and they both stayed until dusk doing what they could to help.

By the time they eventually got back to the vineyard it was too dark to see what kind of state everything was in. And neither of them were ready to face any more that night. At his tentative suggestion that he should go round the vineyard and assess the damage, Tara said, 'You've been terrific Tom, but there's no way I'm going to let you take a torch out to the fields tonight. Whatever state it's in we can't do anything now, so we may as well wait until tomorrow.'

But she did not know the full extent of the havoc wrought to the vines. Or what else tomorrow was going to bring!

6

In the morning, when Tara turned on her bedroom radio, there was a news item about the freak weather in the West Country. The newsreader said that the village of Tamary Hollow had suffered more than anywhere else in the area. Local residents, according to reports, were stunned by the extent of the devastation and were taking stock.

Insurance companies were likely to be paying out many thousands, trees were uprooted and roofers, tree fellers and plumbers were being urgently summoned to repair the havoc the storm had wrought.

Tara was up early, but she didn't go outdoors, or even look out of the window, until Tom and some of the others arrived. She knew she must face it soon but it just wasn't something she could bear to do alone. She told herself that she would wait for company — on the premise that a trouble shared is a trouble halved!

When Tom came, with two of the part-timers, he was white-faced and they were all looking grim. They'd not been able to avoid seeing some of the damage on their way to the cottage, and a pall of gloom hung over them.

She looked at Tom and was almost afraid to ask. Finally she swallowed hard and said, 'Is it bad?'

He nodded. 'Afraid so. About as bad as it could get.'

They walked round the vineyard in procession and none of them said very much. There wasn't much to say. Wind-beaten, drenched, wires downed and stakes awry, the vines presented a sorry sight. It was heartbreaking. So much hard work had gone into this crop, so much preparation, so many high hopes. It seemed monstrous that it could all come to nothing.

Tara, guiltily conscious that she didn't need it for her livelihood, still felt as though a precious gift had been torn away. As for Tom, it was his pride and joy that had been ruined. Not just one year's work but the culmination of the other years in which he had been steadily adding new strains and better husbandry. He had had hopes of a result that would be worthy of everything he had put in. Not to mention a secret belief that Tara would eventually come round to some of the innovations that he, like Ben Lavalle, was convinced would be of such immense benefit. In one hour of bad weather all that was dashed. He was sure she would be ruined.

'It's hopeless,' he said, after a while, as they came to the end of their inspection. 'There's virtually nothing to salvage. Mostly because of the hail-stones. They've ripped up the growing shoots, and struck the early grapes. Any worth salvaging would develop now with broken skins. It would mean mould and that would produce a wine with a flavour no-one would want

— and that we couldn't, in all fairness, even try to sell.' He rubbed his head with a tired hand and repeated again, 'It's hopeless.'

Tara attempted to console him. 'Well never say die. There're always risks like this to wine growing. I know it's dreadful that we'd had such a calamity this year but we'll succeed next year. Nothing like this would happen again. The vines will fruit again next year. Lightning can't possibly strike twice in the same place.'

'Can't it? I wouldn't be too sure of that.' Tom's usual cheeriness had disappeared completely. He was looking at her curiously. 'You mean you're willing to start all over next year? Frankly, Tara, are you sure you can afford it?'

Tara rushed to reassure them all, but specifically Tom. 'There's no need to worry about that. I've had a good year at — at the business in London — none of you will lose your jobs.'

She said to Tom, 'Could we talk?'

and, at his nod, led the way back to the cottage.

Once they were alone she said, 'I'm so sorry, Tom. It's worse for you than for anyone. But there's no question of giving up or packing it in. Believe me I can carry the loss, and the expenses, for one more year. As long as you don't mind going through it all again.' Privately she was thinking that she would, in fact, be more strapped for cash flow than she was pretending. Which made it all the more important she should get on with the paintings and have enough work assembled to provide Derek with the basis of a successful exhibition.

Tom shook his head. He sighed and said heavily. 'It wasn't just the job. I wouldn't like you to think that.'

'I know.' Tara said it sympathetically but she wasn't sure whether he meant the vines crop or his interest in her. She hoped devoutly that it was the former and that there would never again be any mention of the latter! Tom had taken his rejection well and she was anxious they should stay on the friendly terms they had quickly re-established.

He said curiously, 'I still find it hard to believe you can cope with this — moneywise I mean.'

'I can. You must just accept it.' Tara spoke sharply. The last thing she wanted was too much probing into the course of her finances. That would be treading on dangerous ground.

She said briskly, 'The best — and only — thing to do now is to clear everything up and see how we can best limit the damage.'

Tom took the hint immediately and rose to his feet. 'I'll get everyone on to that straightaway. It'll be good for us all to have work to do. Thanks for everything, Tara. The reassurance about their jobs was just what they needed.'

And you needed that, too, Tara thought, she said nothing more, simply giving him an encouraging smile as he left, pleased that he was looking more cheerful and optimistic.

Once Tom was out of sight her smile slipped. She had kept up a cheerful facade for everyone's sake but the sight of her lovely little vineyard in such devastation had, in reality, upset her badly. Now, with no-one to see or hear, she could indulge her genuine feelings about it.

With both hands in front of her face, her shoulders began to shake as the held back tears welled over the edge of her eyes. Even as she scolded herself for being ridiculous — she had no right to cry about a crop, but try as she would to remind herself that many people in the village had far more to worry about, and what a blessing it was that no-one had been hurt there was still an overwhelming need to give way to feelings of grief and loss.

When the kitchen door opened, she was making too much noise herself and too wrapped up in her own private world to see or hear the man who came in. A silent figure, tall and looming, he stood by the door and took in the scene before him. The girl sitting at the table, her head down on her arms, her shoulders shaking with sobs. His rather stern face softened. Then, acting purely upon the instinct to comfort, he moved forward. The first intimation for Tara, that there was anyone else present, was when she felt his arms go round her, as she was lifted and drawn against a large and solid chest.

At first, just for a moment, she resisted, then, after a surprised glance upwards she allowed herself to be tightly hugged. Was it crazy to feel as though she had come home — that she was where she belonged? Well, crazy or not, just for this moment of need she would simply accept that he was here and she was in his arms. Whatever the future held, whatever had made him go — or come back — questions about that could wait.

In spite of her tangled emotions regarding the man himself, she knew that all he was trying to do was help someone in trouble. Nevertheless, it was wonderfully relaxing to lean her head against the broad shoulder so conveniently to hand and let her emotions run their course.

Presently, the crying stopped. She quietened down and Ben, with a smile, offered her a box of tissues from her own kitchen counter. She blew her nose vigorously and looked up at him through watery and slightly ashamed eyes. His rare smile was intimate, even affectionate.

'Feeling better now?'

'Yes, thanks. I'm sorry to be such an idiot.'

'I don't think you're being idiotic at all. I've seen what has happened to the vineyard. Anyone would be upset.'

Ben had not moved away, they were still very close. He said, 'I was on the way back anyway. I heard about it on the car radio. They said nobody in the village had been hurt. It's a miracle if that's true. It is, isn't it?'

'Yes, thank goodness. But there's a lot of property damaged and the old oak's down. Just imagine, it's been standing there for a hundred years and now it's gone. The roots sticking up in the air looked horrible — like a felled giant. Yesterday night — it was like war films I've seen — everyone was in shock but all helping everyone else.'

Ben said gravely. 'That's what living in a small community is all about. Pulling together. They're good people.'

'Yes they are.' Tara was grateful for his understanding, his appreciation of something she took very seriously.

Ben put his hands on her upper arms, holding her in front of him. He was looking down into her face. 'Are you all right now?'

She was suddenly conscious of her appearance at such close quarters. She put agitated fingers to her rumpled hair and wiped the back of her hands across her still wet cheeks. 'I must look frightful.'

Something quite different from sympathy had come into Ben's expression. He was gazing at her as though seeing her for the first time. 'You're wrong.' he said softly, almost wonderingly. 'You look beautiful — truly beautiful — and very different from the girl I first met in the moonlight.'

Tara said nothing. The moment was too precious, and she was afraid to break the spell. But perhaps her big eyes said it for her. Ben's own eyes roamed her face, and his hands began pulling her gently back towards him.

When he bent his head towards her, Tara knew, with absolute certainty, that this kiss was a very different matter from the angry grab he had made on the evening they had met. Or the incident in her cottage on his first visit there. This time he was kissing Tara, someone he knew and liked, someone for whom he had acquired respect.

When the kiss ended they were both shaken. There was conscious embarrassment when their eyes met again.

Ben looked as if, for once, he was uncertain of himself.

Tara couldn't help herself when she

moved in his slackened grasp, got her arms free, and put them around his neck. His own arms tightened in response and the pressure on her lips returned. There was unexpected sweetness in his kiss, yet the gentleness lasted only as long as it took for him to become swayed by her response. After that their embrace changed to one of consuming passion.

Tara was first to break free, and draw back. When he would have possessed her lips again, she put up a hand in front of his mouth and said, laughingly, 'Please, Ben. I've got to think for a minute.'

He let her go at once, but his look was devouring and eager. Tara, feeling that this meeting after so long, should have developed on different lines, moved away across the room on the other side of the kitchen table. 'This is a fine thing. Staying away without a word and coming back to — to . . . '

'To what?' Ben's look dared her to name it. His dark eyes had the sort of warmth in them she had thought never to see in these particular eyes.

Tara said, 'I'll make you some coffee.' She was still breathless but it was as much from the excitement, the electricity, between them as from the embrace.

Ben dropped down into a kitchen chair. He said quizzically, 'I rather think you're trying to take my mind off other things.'

'I am.' Tara put the kettle on and sat down opposite him. He immediately took her hand. The contact was pleasurable, the sense of intimacy great, but she tried to concentrate on what she meant to say. 'You didn't ring — or write — or let me know when you were going. I just woke up one day and you weren't here.' She realised that she was making it sound reproachful and was regretful immediately she'd said it. After all, what right did she have to question his movements?

'No.' Ben had let go her hand and moved restlessly in his chair. 'I didn't know it would matter to you. To be honest, I didn't even know it would matter to me. But it did. I missed you.' He leaned across the table and kissed her lightly on the tip of her nose. Tara laughed. She felt heady and exultant. Whatever he'd done, whatever he'd gone away to do, surely she couldn't be wrong about him, surely he was basically good.

She was at pains not to let him know the extent of her exhilaration. 'We were busy anyway,' she said, and a shadow of remembrance crossed her face. How incredible that in the excitement of finding each other she had temporarily forgotten what had happened to the vineyard.

'Can I stay for a while. I know there isn't any work but it doesn't matter. I'd just like to stay in Tamary,' Ben said.

Tara thought he meant with her, and hestitated. If he expected to stay in the cottage with her, it was going much too fast for her. She was not prepared for that kind of commitment.

He saw her hesitation and said

immediately. 'At the inn of course.'

'Oh.' Tara blushed. He knew what she had thought and was smiling. She said, 'It's nothing to do with me is it. I can hardly prevent you.'

'You're wrong. It has a great deal to do with you.' Ben's look was meaningful and Tara's gaze dropped before it. She rose quickly and went across to the counter to busy herself with making and serving the coffee.

As they drank he asked about Tom and how he had taken the loss of the vines. Tara sighed, 'He was pretty devastated but he'd cheered up when he left here with Len and Harry. Once they knew I wasn't going to sell up or abandon the vineyard they were all relieved, I think.'

Ben said, 'Can you really afford to start again?'

'Yes.' Tara was uncomfortable. She said crisply, in a decisive, close-the-subject voice. 'That's definite,' and gave him a defiant look.

Ben looked at her curiously but was

perceptive enough to see her unwilling-
ness to be questioned. Instead he got to
his feet. 'I'll go and see Tom. Offer him
my commiserations.' At the door he
turned. 'Are you in tonight?'

Tara wondered why it was she was
suddenly breathless again. She tried not
to show the excitement, the anticipation
that was coursing through her. 'Yes.'
Striving for a casual air she enquired,
'How would you fancy chicken risotto?'

He smiled. 'Great. But what I really
fancy is spending time with you.'

Tara smiled back. Long after he had
gone, the smile still lingered on. It was
hard to remember that she had started
the day in misery.

7

Whatever her anticipation of the evening, the reality was as good — and better.

The Ben who arrived at the cottage late that night was everything she could have wished — warm, intelligent, teasing, appreciative. It was a heady excitement to find the real man who had been concealed behind the dour facade for so long. Something inside Tara, an inner knowledge, had always known he could be like this.

Unselfconsciously, in response to the letting down of some of his guard, she showed him the real Tara. Even though Tamara was still her secret! Together they had an evening of mutual delight in each other. And in a situation neither of them had expected, and both were still surprised had come about. They ate a little, drank a little and talked quite a lot! Although the talk still had reservations! By tacit consent neither ventured onto forbidden territory. So no mention was made of the past, or why Tara had been so unwilling to change her methods of running her vineyard, or where her money came from. Nothing was said about where Ben had been during his absence — or why he was unwilling to live in France.

The thought did cross Tara's mind, rather forlornly, that she wished he would trust her and confide in her. It would have made it so much easier for her to tell him about her secret identity — and confess that she had painted a portrait of him.

Nevertheless, in spite of the fact that he gave her no explanations about himself, she was still content — for the present. The feeling between them was too good, too exciting, for her to be anything else.

All through the evening there had been moments of heightened awareness between them. A sparkling look, a touch of the hand that set one or the other on fire, even a light kiss on her brow. Before he came, she had wondered whether he would try to make love to her — and, if he did, what her own reaction would be!

Just as he was leaving, he held out his arms and said, with a catch in his voice, 'Come here, Tara.'

She did not hesitate but went to be enfolded in them like a child coming gratefully home. His beard tickled her hair deliciously, as she snuggled up to him.

He said, his mouth moving on her forehead, 'Thank you for a wonderful dinner, Tara.'

He gazed down, his mouth curved in a smile, his eyes saying things his stubborn mouth found hard to express. 'Tomorrow,' he promised, 'it's my turn to provide you with a meal. I'm taking you to that little restaurant on the road to Exeter two miles out of the village — and I'm going to wine and dine you suitably.'

Tara said demurely, 'I'm afraid I already have a date,' and instantly felt him stiffen alarmingly. 'Ben, don't, I'm joking,' she said hastily, frightened by the speed with which his warmth had turned to immobile rigidity.

Slowly his mouth, tightened to a straight line, loosened up again. He said, 'I'm sorry, that was silly of me. Of course you were. I thought . . . it's just . . . '

'It's just what?' Tara prompted him.

The answer, when it came, seemed forced out of him. 'It's just that I find it hard to trust a woman.'

She wondered bitterly who the woman was who had caused him so much pain. And suffered pain herself at being described by him simply as 'a woman'. But she said nothing, simply waited, instinctively aware that this was the first chink of light into what made Ben Lavalle such an enigma. He was half-apologising for a perceived character fault he saw in himself yet still he offered none of the hoped-for explanations.

Instead he looked down at her again and the light came on in his eyes once more, as though a switch had been pulled.

'In a minute I'm going out of that door. I don't trust myself to stay any longer,' he said huskily. 'But I'm going to do this.' And he took her head gently between his hands and kissed her.

Tara savoured the moment. As before, the embrace began gently, lovingly, and became more urgent as their lips explored.

Ben pulled away and let her go so abruptly that she almost felt lost in a strange empty land. He was at the door before she had fully opened her eyes, and she felt a growing loss at no longer being in his arms. 'Good-night until tomorrow.'

And with that, he was gone.

On the following evening Ben called for her at seven o'clock. They had met during the day but only in the company of others. When the Saab drew up outside, he was more formally dressed than she was used to seeing him, and her heart swelled with pride.

As they entered the restaurant she heard an older woman remark to her husband, 'What a handsome pair that couple make.'

They looked like a couple did they? That was how it felt too! Tara, looking at him, hoped passionately that her portrait had been successful in catching that particular devil-may-care expression. He was a different man tonight from the dour one of earlier days.

When they returned to the cottage, Tara said, 'Would you like to come in for a coffee?'

Ben hesitated. They were still in the car. He took a hand off the steering wheel and laid it over hers. His look was grave, and held a question. 'Is that wise?'

Tara did not pretend to misunderstand. Her hand turned under his and was clasped. She said steadily, 'I'd like you to.'

126

Their gazes locked and Ben smiled, as he said, 'I would love to.'

In the living-room, she had just put a tray of coffee down on the small table, when the phone rang. Ben glanced at his watch. 'It's half past ten. Rather late for someone to be ringing you.'

Tara frowned. 'Yes. I can't imagine who it is. Excuse me.' She went into the hall and picked up the receiver.

It was Derek. His voice held over-tones of uncharacteristic irritation. 'Sorry, Tara. I haven't heard from you and things are getting very difficult at this end. You know the date, my dear, you really should have been in touch. I've tried to get you several times without success. Things are urgent. I've booked the gallery for the exhibition and we don't have a lot of time. We simply must consult at the earliest possible moment.'

'I understand.' Tara felt guilty on two counts. She had been neglecting her career and avoiding contact with Derek. She was also acutely conscious of the quiet cottage and the fact that her replies could be heard in the living-room.

'Just a moment,' she said and went back to the door. Ben looked up as she put her head round it. He was frowning slightly and raised his eyebrows in enquiry. 'It's a London call,' she said, rather nervously, aware that her other life was still virtually unknown to him. It felt wrong to be having secrets from him but she had no choice. 'I'll try to make it as short as possible.'

He gave a nod and Tara was back to the phone. Derek was getting impatient and insisted that she should come up as soon as possible. He was helpless, so he said, to continue with arrangements until they had been able to liase. 'Tomorrow would be best.'

'Tomorrow?' Tara was horrified. The last thing she wanted was to go away just when Ben and she seemed to have found each other. Nonetheless, she knew Derek was right. It had to be done — and perhaps it would be better to go and get it over. Then she could return and be more settled until just before the exhibition itself.

'All right,' she heard herself reluctantly agreeing. 'If I've really got to come, then tomorrow it shall be. I'll arrive in the early afternoon. But understand that I can't stay long. Just a couple of days — long enough for us to sort things out and make plans.'

'Great!' Derek sounded relieved. 'I was afraid you were going to say you hadn't got enough done and we were going to have to cancel.'

Tara said honestly. 'Well, there isn't much — but I can't afford not to. Am I staying with you?'

'Of course. Jo's got your room all ready.' Derek was happy at having got her agreement. 'Sweet dreams, Tara. See you tomorrow.'

Tara laughed. 'Sweet dreams to you too. Good-night — until tomorrow.' She put down the receiver and returned to the living room.

Ben said heavily, 'Your coffee is cold.'

'It doesn't matter.' Tara sipped slowly looking at him across the rim of her cup. The coffee wasn't half as cold as the atmosphere in the room. Clearly the telephone call had changed the whole mood. Miserably she supposed she had better break the news of her forthcoming trip.

'It was — er — a business contact. He — they — reminded me I was due to go to town for a day or so. I'm sorry I really don't have any choice.'

'No, I'm sure you don't.' Ben drained his cup and set it back on the saucer. He rose to his feet.

'I couldn't help overhearing some of your call,' he said very deliberately. 'I feel sure that with a journey tomorrow you'll need your beauty sleep tonight — so I'll be going now.'

'Oh.' Tara stood up too. What had happened to the rapport they had had earlier in the evening? The telephone call, it seemed, had put an end to everything. There was a glass barrier between them now and she knew instinctively that there was nothing she could do or say that would allow her to reach him. For whatever reason, he had put it there himself — and meant it to keep her at a distance. He did not even kiss her good-night.

She shut the door behind him and went to bed.

When the sound of the car had gone, sleep did not come nearly as easily as it had on the previous evening. Tara kept tossing and turning for hours. Her last conscious thought was a desperate wish to have Ben back again, so that she could confide in him. She would, she vowed, on their very next meeting, tell him everything. Whatever had come between them it was not going to be her fault if the barriers could not be pulled down. No more secrets!

But when she drove up the motorway next morning her eyes were dark-rimmed from fatigue — and anxiety. The anxiety was because she sensed that telling him her secrets might still not be enough to overcome the chasm of distrust between them.

And she didn't know what else she could do . . .

With Tara gone, Ben considered that the cottage looked forlorn and lonely. He and Tom were repairing and painting the outbuildings close by when the fanciful notion came to him. Perhaps it was because of his inability to make his peace with Tara, until she returned. He felt badly about the way he had behaved. But hearing her making an assignation had filled him with impotent fury. In the light of the morning he recognised that there might be some other explanation than the conclusion he had jumped to, that she had lied about still being in touch with Hugh. She had sounded so guilty, so much as though she were making a lame excuse for rushing off to London that all his distrust had re-surfaced. Now he was sorry — and unable to tell her so.

Standing up to stretch an aching back, he said to Tom, 'Can you see something strange about the roof of the cottage?'

Tom looked. 'Right enough, there are slates slipped down. I wonder she's not noticed that. I should think there must be damp inside. I'd better get in and do something about it.'

'You know she's away then?'

'Yes, of course. She left a message for me — and the key.'

'There's not much to do here today, Tom. I'd be glad to put the roof right — could you let me have the key and I'll get in and assess the damage — start on it right away.'

Tom dug into his jacket pocket and silently handed him a key.

'There's another ladder — and tools are in the shed. Just give me a shout if you want any help.'

'I will — and thanks.' Ben gave the other man a straight look — which was returned — and made his way to the cottage. He was whistling as he let himself in and moved towards the stairs. The damaged roof was over the big dormer window. It was in that room he must go to check the ceiling.

He realised that he had never been upstairs. The place was surprisingly big. In Tara's studio he stopped surprised. He didn't know what he had expected but this was a shock. Paintings were stacked against the wall, charming landscapes mostly, all with a distinctive style. There was a scrawled signature at the bottom of each 'Tamara'. Ben stood looking down at them, and a slow smile began to spread across his face. So this was her secret! She was 'Tamara' — the well-known artist. He had been wrong and glad to be so.

Neither Hugh nor some unknown London 'business' was the source of her wealth. She had earned it with her brush — but there was nothing to be ashamed of in that. She had every right to be proud of it, in fact, so why had she been at such pains to hide it? Especially from him!

He got a stepladder and some tools. The hole in the ceiling was not too difficult for him to repair without needing anyone else's assistance. The main thing now was to put the slates back into place — and for that he must get up on the roof from outside.

As he walked back through the studio he caught his foot in the easel. There was a canvas draped over the large picture standing on it. His arms flayed wildly as he fought to keep his balance. The picture toppled sideways and he reached for it, but the covering slipped away.

Holding the portrait between his two hands Ben was turned to stone. At first he could not believe that it was his own face that was looking back at him. Rakish, half-smiling, larger than life, with a distant background painted in of his French chateau and the vines.

'No!' It was a desperate cry of denial. The picture was everything he least wanted. Publicity! He'd had too much already! For a moment he wanted to hurl it to the ground or rip the tools on the floor across the smiling face. Then a cold dislike filled his mind. She had been slyly drawing him all the time. Those times when he had thought she enjoyed his company; those times she had watched his face so carefully, had seemed to take such an interest in his opinions! It had all been for her damned portrait. Everything he had suspected about women was right. They were totally untrustworthy. How could he have begun to believe that Tara was different? Now there was this to prove him wrong. He hung the picture against the wall, then snatched up a sketch pad from the floor and began writing rapidly. There was such anger in him that his pencil deeply indented the paper. He finished with a scrawled signature, folded it, and pinned it to the easel.

Then he returned to Tom. 'Sorry, but I have to go. I've left her a note.' He thrust the key at him, turned, and was gone before Tom could frame a question.

Tom looked up at the roof. The slates were still off. Shaking his head in bewilderment he went towards the shed.

8

As she returned to Devon, Tara's brain buzzed with plans. Derek had given her plenty to think about, and to do! But if her head was in London, her heart was at home in Tamary Hollow — home which now held everything she wanted.

As she approached the village, she saw how the great storm had changed the landscape for ever. Not just the oak, but other familiar trees had gone too. The copse at the top of the hill leading down to the main street had been severely denuded. Branches and trunks were neatly stacked on the ground. The scars would heal over, but it would be a while before the damage was unremarked.

Usually she took pleasure in approaching her cottage from the back — through the vineyard, but today she took the main street route, directly to her front door. Time enough to see the remains of her poor battered vines. Maybe Ben was out there now, still helping Tom clear up the devastation.

The cottage was as welcoming as ever. Mellow sunlight glinted through its windows, catching the polished surfaces of the furniture. It was very quiet and peaceful, but Tara felt a pang of disappointment — irrational of course. Hadn't she just decided that Ben would be out in the fields? He'd no way of knowing her arrival time. But somehow, she'd pictured coming home to the excitement of his arms. Still, she'd think of that as a pleasure to come.

It didn't take her long to unpack, and change into jeans and shirt, thankfully shedding the short, tight skirt and heels she'd worn for London. She made coffee, and took out the list of suggestions and commissions from Derek. There was a lot of work, all of it interesting and stimulating — more so, because now she could share it with

Ben. Driving back, she'd been looking forward to sharing the secret of her identity with him. She wanted to — her painting was still of paramount importance — it always would be, but Ben had invaded her heart, and she couldn't deny him such a major part of her life. She'd worry about the implications later. They'd work that out. The portrait was another matter, but once he knew about her painting, he'd surely accept the portrait, particularly as it was so splendid!

She wanted to go up to the studio to see it — to make certain it was as good as she remembered, but she'd wait — until she'd seen the real Ben, and they could go up together. The desire to see him was overwhelming. It was impossible to settle down to work, and the knowledge of her secret identity began to press down as an intolerable burden. It was strange — she'd always enjoyed the dual identity game before, but hiding things from Ben felt wrong. The way had to be cleared of all misunderstandings and misconceptions. She was desperate to find him, and tell him everything. No more secrets!

The fields had a deserted, abandoned look — like the Marie Celeste, no soul stirred there. Work had been done. Some stakes had been repaired or renewed, patches of vines had been saved, but whole areas were still flattened, the sprawling plants already withering, their fruit rotting. Tara looked away. It was a sad battlefield. But she remembered some comforting words Ben had said — 'nothing is forever . . .'

There were signs of life at last! Tom emerged from one of the sheds, his face lighting with pleasure as he saw her. 'Tara, you're back! It seems an age . . .'

'Only a couple of days.'

'It feels like longer. We haven't been able to do much here yet. I was waiting to talk to you — about the future.' The look he gave her was ambiguous.

Tara replied hurriedly, 'I'm sorry, I haven't had time yet . . . It's been hectic in London.' Then the question, burning in her head. Casually, she asked, 'Where is everybody? Is Ben around?'

'No. I've rescued as many vines as I could. That didn't take long, I'm afraid. No, Ben's not here.'

'Oh — where is he then?'

Tom looked at her curiously. 'He's gone.'

'Gone!' Tara's heart contracted. 'Where to? When will he be back?' Fear started to gather.

Tom shrugged. 'I've no idea. He went off suddenly. No word of warning. In fact we still owe him some money.'

'He'll be back then?'

'Shouldn't think so. It was only a day or so's wages, and he never showed much interest in his pay packet. Rather a mystery man, our Ben. I always thought he'd take off again some day. Didn't expect it to be so soon, though.'

'But didn't he say anything — anything at all? No message for me?' The fear had turned to ice now — a slow seeping numbness. She shivered.

'Are you all right, Tara? You look a bit strange.'

'It's OK . . . it's just . . . When did you last see Ben?'

'Just after you'd gone. He was a bit moody the morning you left. Then we noticed the slates on the cottage roof. There was quite a hole over that big window you had cut into the gable. Ben went up to take a look. He needed to fix it from the inside first, so he went into the house. We'd been doing some maintenance work on the sheds. I carried on. Suddenly he came out, looking thunderous, hardly said a word, and drove off for good. I think he said he'd left a note for you. He'd repaired the hole but the slates still needed putting back. I went up on the roof and finished the job. You'll need to check later.'

'Thanks.' The word came from frozen lips. She turned and ran back into the cottage.

'Tara, we need to talk . . . ' Tom's words were lost as she slammed the

142

back door and raced upstairs, knowing already what she'd find there.

The studio looked exactly as always, apart from two things. A damp patch on the ceiling showed the storm damage. That was of little importance. What mattered was the portrait — and the note. The portrait had been moved, the piratical face turned away, as close to the wall as possible, as though someone — Ben, of course — wished to annihilate it, but couldn't bring himself actually to destroy it. The note was pinned to the easel. Tara read it — every scathing word struck ice into her heart. So this was the end.

'Tara!' Tom's voice floated up the stairway.

She dropped the note on the floor, locked the door, and went down to meet him.

'Hey, you aren't well, are you? You're quite white. Tara,' he spoke sharply now, anxiety snagging his voice, 'sit down, you're trembling.' He led her to a chair.

With a tremendous effort she spoke, trying to keep her voice as normal as possible. 'I'm all right, Tom, really. It must be a bug of some sort. Probably picked it up in London. Food poisoning,' she invented wildly, wishing desperately he'd go away, and leave her alone to absorb her misery and give way to her feelings. 'Please, Tom, I'll be better on my own. I'll go to bed, have a sleep. We'll talk about the vineyard tomorrow.'

'I can't leave you like this, you need looking after. I'll get you some tea.'

'No! Please, Tom, go away. I just want to be on my own. I hate being ill. I hate, even more, being fussed over. Please.'

'Well, if you're sure . . . '

Tara closed her eyes. 'I'm sure.'

He still hung about, reluctant to go, but finally she heard the door click to, and she was free to go back to the studio.

Numbness was a kind of anaesthesia for a while. She turned the portrait around to face her, and with her critical artist's eye, saw that it was very good indeed. She had captured that elusive ambivalence that summed up Ben Lavalle. But even as she'd found that quality in the image, she'd lost the man himself. He was gone from her life and she knew he'd gone for good.

After the numbness came the hurt that he'd left so abruptly, especially after their last few times together. Thinking of his warmth and tenderness when she'd been so upset, hurt gave way to anger. Anger that he hadn't stayed to let her explain, and that he'd lumped her in with all women — betrayers and deceivers. Anger was useful, crowding out other, more painful, emotions. Pride surfaced too. She'd been hurt before — and had recovered. At least she still had her painting. Concentrated work would be the best antidote to unhappiness. Avoiding the dark eyes of Ben's protrait, she picked it up and, just as he had done, turned its face to the wall,

145

but this time, in the furthest corner of the room, well away from the easel.

Throughout the days that followed, Tara tried desperately hard to rid Ben from her mind. She set herself a vigorous timetable, working on her landscapes until the light faded. Evenings were the worst times. With nothing to occupy her, her mind sneakily let in memories of evenings when Ben was around the cottage after work. Somehow her village friends weren't, at present, the company she needed. Tom frequently asked her out, but she always found an excuse to refuse.

Then something else began to happen — something deeply worrying to her — more worrying than anything that had happened in her working life before. She'd been concentrating on landscapes because, among Derek's suggestions for the exhibition, was a request for some new ones. Countryside scenes were the most popular 'bread and butter' items, and stocks were low.

'We need at least a dozen,' Derek had said. 'You know the sort of thing — thatched cottages, stone bridges, picnic spot scenes — to remind people of summer and all the imagined golden days of long ago.'

She'd laughed then. 'Are you implying that my pictures are pure fantasies?'

'No, no. It's just that there's a reassuring serenity about them. Makes people feel secure, happy. I expect it's because you're at ease with yourself in the country, and you communciate it through your pictures. It's a quality unique to Tamara.'

Landscapes were the easiest of all things to Tara and, in a way, the reason she'd switched to portraits was that she felt she needed the challenge. It was much harder to capture an expression, a soul in the eyes, a character in the shape of the mouth; a face was an ever-changing map, its contours shifting and resettling endlessly. The landscape stayed more or less stable long enough for her to depict it.

For a couple of days, she drove around the countryside, marking potential spots. The vineyard, she left to Tom, simply telling him to clear and repair as much as he could. Its long term future, she'd think about later. It was bound up with memories of Ben, whereas her country scenes had nothing to do with him — that side of her life was hers alone.

And that was her terrible error, but it was some time before she'd admit it. Well away from Tamary Hollow, she found a charming cluster of cottages near a village green which even had a traditional pump. She made preliminary sketches, noted colours, and took them home to the studio. It didn't take her long to put it together, but it didn't please her. She tore up her first effort and started again. It was no good. The painting ws technically satisfactory, but it was too dull, had no life in it. She put it on one side, and started the next.

A river scene. A pretty arched bridge, a willow tree sweeping the banks, sunlight filtering through the clear water to shimmer on brown stones and pebbles in the riverbed. The sort of tranquil, calming scene she loved. Everything was perfect except that it wouldn't come right. She couldn't get the sunlit effect — the brown water was muddy. In the studio, trying again, her eyes were constantly drawn to the portrait in the corner. Its blank back mocked her. 'Damn — damn him.' She was terrified to find it was her voice which had yelled out.

She left the studio. Fortunately the weather was fine and she could work outside — on site. She thought she'd found the answer, but when she brought the sketches home, they too were lack-lustre and ordinary.

It got worse, and she began to lose her confidence, sitting, staring for hours at blank paper, unable even to execute the preliminary work.

The date of the exhibition loomed nearer. Panic, like some beast on her shoulders, threatened to consume her entirely. She phoned Derek. 'Something terrible's happened.' Her voice was high, unnatural.

'Tara, what's the matter. You sound odd.'

'Derek — I can't — I can't paint any more.' Although it was a relief to admit it finally, it brought leaden despair with it.

There was a long pause. 'Have you been overdoing it lately?'

'That's the problem — I can't paint at all. What am I going to do?'

A rising note of hysteria alerted Derek to the seriousness of the call. 'Don't worry, Tara. It happens. A block of some kind. Come up to stay with us. Have a rest before the exhibition.'

'But you don't understand. I can't do the exhibition. I haven't enough to exhibit. Well — a few scenes — but they're rubbish. I can't show them.'

'I'll be the judge of that, Tara. Don't be foolish. You can't just walk away from this. No, listen,' he pre-empted her strangled protests. 'Bring everything you can lay your hands on up here. What about the portrait you told me about? You were excited enough about that.'

'I can't . . . ' Tara started to say, then thought, why can't I? The last thing she wanted in the cottage was a reminder of Ben Lavalle. And she knew the picture was excellent. It would maintain her status in the art world — there was no question about that.'

'And, Tara, lay off for a day or two. Come up here to stay, just for a break. We'd love to have you. Forget about painting. It'll come back in its own good time.'

'I hope so! I won't come yet, thanks Derek. I've got to keep on trying. There's just not enough to mount a full exhibition.'

'That doesn't need to be a problem. I've got one or two proteges who'd give their eye teeth to have something of theirs in a Tamara exhibition.'

'All right. I'll do what I can,' she promised before continuing, 'I'll come

151

up a couple of days before. I don't want to leave Tamary for too long.'

'Why not?' Derek's voice was bland, but he knew Tara well, and sensed that it was more than her attachment to her country haven that made her reluctant to leave it.

'Oh — just — there's still the vineyard to think about. There's a lot to do. See you soon then, and love to Jo.'

She went to the window and stared unseeingly over her fields. There was a lot to do, but Tom was capable of doing most of it. What she couldn't acknowledge, even to her own heart, the reason she didn't want to leave Tamary Hollow — was the hope that Ben Lavalle might return.

9

'I've seen that face before, but I can't recall where.' Derek moved back a few steps, a frown of concentration lining his forehead.

'It's a fantastic portrait,' Jo said, 'and I think it looks familiar because it's archetypical. Quite a few people have that 'I am in the present but really I belong in the past' sort of face. He must be a modern romantic from Tara's imagination — her dream man, I'd say.'

'Nonsense,' Derek retorted. 'I know him. It'll come to me. Maybe without the beard . . . ' He went close to the picture, and covered the lower part of Ben's face. He shook his head. 'No, but I'll get it eventually. You're right, Jo, it's one of Tara's best pieces. The sitter is real, I take it? Not someone from your imagination?'

'He's real all right,' Tara said, rather

wishing he wasn't. Life would be so much easier if Ben had been a figment of her imagination. Then she'd know for sure that he was beyond her reach in reality.

'I don't suppose you'll tell me who he is?' Derek looked hopeful.

'I can't. He doesn't know it's in the exhibition.'

'Isn't that a bit risky?' Jo looked worried.

'I don't think so. I don't ever expect to see him again. It's my property anyway.'

'It is for sale?'

'I'm not . . . '

Derek interrupted her as a young man came into the gallery. 'Ah, here's Bryn. He's been dying to meet you.'

Derek, Jo, and Tara were having a drink before the exhibition opened. With just half an hour to go, Tara felt the usual nerves beginning to flutter in her stomach. Usually it was with excitement, but not this time. In spite of the keyed-up tension of opening day, the dull grey despair that had settled on her life showed no sign of lifting.

The portrait, however, was undoubtedly a masterpiece, standing out from the rest of the paintings. Derek had been kind about her new landscapes, but she knew he was disappointed in them.

'Oh, they'll sell, probably to new clients, but for anyone interested in building up a 'Tamara' collection, I'm afraid they'll be waiting for the next show. But,' he hurried on, seeing her crestfallen face, 'you mustn't worry. It'll come back. Yours is too large a talent for it just to disappear. Has anything happened? Personally, I mean, in your life. Anything else wrong at Tamary Hollow? Is the cleaning up operation going well?'

'Yes, of course.' Tara, frightened of the shrewd questioning in Derek's eyes, rushed to change the subject. 'I do like Bryn's pictures. How did you get hold of him?'

'Usual channels. I thought it best to

find a back-up after what you told me. A combination of 'experienced artist and beginner.' He's a mountain land-scape man, so it's a good contrast.'

Bryn Evans now approached the small group, shyly holding out his hand to Tara. 'You're Tamara. I can't tell you how pleased I am to be exhibiting my paintings with you — beyond my wildest dreams.'

'Don't be so modest. Your pictures are very good. I love the Scottish ski-scapes. You've exactly caught the light and shades.'

Bryn's eyes caught the portrait of Ben. 'Did you do that?'

'She did. Do you know him?' Derek asked.

'No. At least I don't think so. It's kind of — well — intriguing. The sort of face you can't stop looking at, wondering about . . . '

Don't I know it, Tara thought sadly.

'If the mutual admiration society's over, you've just about enough time for a drink.' Derek poured champagne in a fourth glass, and raised his own. 'Let the show begin, in exactly . . . ' he looked at his watch, ' . . . two and a half minutes from now.'

Tara looked around, and shifted uncomfortably from one foot to the other, wishing she was back in Tamary Hollow, remembering why she loved it so much there! Her first exhibitions had been fun, for then she'd been making a name for herself. Now, she'd much rather have left the selling to Derek. 'If someone's spending a lot of money on a painting, they've a right to meet the painter,' he'd always insisted.

Tara remembered her youthful chirpiness then. 'How about a Van Gogh?' she'd said.

Derek had looked at her sternly. 'The day you're in that bracket, young lady, I shall be able to retire to my own Caribbean island.'

Now, as a successful artist, she was less cocky. Some would-be purchases had spoken to her, and former clients too, but she noticed that several of

Bryn's paintings were already sporting red stickers, while her own sales were comparatively few.

Bryn came over to her during a lull. 'Do you want a drink, Tara? It's going well, isn't it?'

She smiled at him. 'No thanks. I'll wait until it's over, and yes, you're doing really well. I'm glad for you.' She didn't want to dampen his spirits but privately she'd always considered that at least three quarters of the people milling about were simply there for a social outing — a chance to see and be seen in the Art World. The well dressed, affluent looking crowd, buzzing with animated chatter, couldn't all be art lovers!

A particular little knot of people in the centre of the room were downing champagne as though prohibition was about to be introduced. Their attention was centred, not on the gallery walls, but on a very beautiful woman who was, not only exquisitely and fashionably dressed, but whose flashing jewellery

158

must have been worth a small fortune. She hadn't been there very long, but seemed to have attracted quite a collection of male followers.

Her laughter carried across the room, and Tara heard her say, 'I really must look at these pictures. I have such a lot of wall to fill at the new flat.'

Tara hoped it wasn't her pictures which would be 'useful to cover' the woman's walls.

The woman examined one or two landscapes, and moved nearer to Tara, who could see now the flawless perfection of her make-up, and the sleek blue-black hair style. She moved towards the portrait, and as she looked at it, Tara saw an incredulous frown creasing the perfect mask. Her cry of surprise was shrill. 'It can't be. What on earth is he doing here?' She spun round, breaking the close ranks of her entourage. 'Where's the artist? Find the gallery owner.'

A couple of men scuttled off through the crowd, but Tara stepped forward in front of the portrait. 'I'm the artist. Tara Cresswell. What's the problem?'

The woman looked her up and down, her mouth tightening. Then she turned to Ben's picture. 'Would you mind stepping aside. I can't see it properly.'

Reluctantly, Tara did so, irritated by the peremptory bossiness in the woman's tone. 'Is anything the matter?' she asked again, as the woman stooped again to peer closely at the picture.

Stepping back, she threw a hard look of dislike at Tara. 'You know the sitter well?'

'Not really. He's just someone who came to stay in the area where I live. I wanted to paint him.'

'And did he agree?'

Tara hesitated. 'Not exactly. He didn't know anything about it,' she admitted.

'Ah!' The exclamation was maliciously triumphant. 'I thought not.'

'Do you know him?' Tara hated to ask.

'I should think so. I've been married

to him for the past ten years.'

Tara put her hands on the wall behind her, looking for something solid to touch. Ben — married! And to this woman. It was a nightmare. She tried to smile, to appear entirely unconcerned, and normal. 'Quite a coincidence,' she managed. 'Is he here too?' She prayed that he wasn't.

'No. This is hardly Ben's sort of thing. I'm Helen Lavalle. I'd like to know when this was painted.' Her light blue eyes were like tempered steel, and high spots of colour stained her peachy make-up.

'I don't think you have any right to know. Isn't that his business?'

'I've every right. I've told you, I'm his wife.'

'Is he with you now?'

'No, but he has been to London. Where was this painted — apparently without his permission?' Her tone was threatening, and most of her admirers had melted away, sensing trouble.

'In Devon. He came down, looking

for work.' Tara's voice was low. She didn't want to talk to this woman about Ben.

Helen Lavalle looked at her shrewdly. She was no fool, and Tara had given herself away immediately she'd heard Ben was married. Helen suspected her of being some kind of threat who needed to be warned off. 'You know who he is, of course,' she said coolly.

Tara shook her head. 'I never asked, and he never told me anything about himself.'

'No wonder. He's hardly likely to be proud of a two year prison sentence — for fraud! You obviously knew nothing about it.' A sigh of mock sympathy rang in Tara's ears. 'That's just like Ben. He always did like to make things difficult. I can see that he took you in completely. Too bad of him . . . '

At that point, while Tara waited for feeling to return to her body, one of Helen's young men returned with Derek in tow. He looked uneasily from

Tara to Helen, standing on either side of Ben's portrait. Afterwards, Derek would always swear that the eyes in the picture held a look of amused contempt which hadn't been there before.

'Problems?' He stepped forward.

'There could be. Were you aware that this artist has painted, and you, as the gallery owner, are exhibiting, my husband's portrait without his — our — permission?'

'And you are?' Derek was politely smooth.

'Helen Lavalle. That — is my husband, Ben Lavalle.'

Derek clapped his hand to his forehead. 'Of course it is. Ben Lavalle. I read about the case. Wasn't he — er — didn't he . . . '

'No need to beat about the bush. After all, he's served his prison sentence now.' Magnaminously, she added, 'I've forgiven him, though at the time . . . ' she sighed, ' . . . it was hard.'

'Tara,' Derek turned to her, 'didn't you know who he was?'

'No, and I still don't know what you're talking about.' But she was horribly sure it was true. Remembering their first meeting, his demanding lips, his pallor, his brooding bitterness. Why hadn't he told her?

'There was a terrific scandal at the time. Thousands of pounds mysteriously went missing. Ben Lavalle was blamed, though the evidence was circumstancial and the sentence light.'

Light! Tara thought with a wave of pity. Two years locked up — for a man like Ben! It crossed her mind to wonder agonisingly whether he really had inherited a fortune from his 'aunt' or if his story had just been a cover.

Derek was examining the portrait again. 'I see now, of course. It's the beard, and he looks older too. There were lots of pictures in the press at the time. I don't remember any of you,' he said to Helen.

'No. Ben specifically asked me to keep out of the limelight. Although, of course, I supported him to the hilt.'

'Really?' Derek looked puzzled. 'I seem to remember that . . . '

Helen cut in hurriedly. 'The point at issue is whether you have a right to exhibit this portrait at all.'

'Oh, I think you'll find we have,' Derek replied easily. 'In any case, I'm sure Mr Lavalle would be reasonable. If you'll give me your husband's phone number, I'll phone him right away. He's not with you today then?'

'No.'

'No.'

Tara and Helen and spoken together. Derek raised his eyebrows at the vehemence of their responses.

Tara faltered, 'I'm not sure it would be a good idea, Derek. Why don't we just withdraw it, if that would satisfy Mrs Lavalle.'

'No. I think the subject of the portrait should be contacted,' Derek persisted. 'After all, it's quite a coup, being painted by Tamara. The picture will have great future value.'

Helen shrugged, and Tara cast her

eyes heavenwards. She was beyond caring what happened to her, or what Ben's reactions would be. As Helen Lavalle had pointed out, she was his wife, and it could be no possible concern of Tara's. For a moment, she felt like ripping the picture to pieces — that would put a final end to the whole episode. Perhaps then, she could forget him, and start painting again. But how could the man she knew have married a woman as shallow as the one before her?

Helen was saying, 'Ben can't be contacted right now. He's in France, at his family home, where we're going to live. Ben's there now, getting it ready for me. That's why I popped in here, to pick up a few water colours to remind us of England. What a co-incidence to find my husband's portrait here, and that the two of you know each other. It's awfully strange that he never mentioned you.' Her smile, directed on Tara, might well have been a poisoned dart with a warmth factor of zero.

Tara couldn't stand it any longer. Let them sort the portrait out between them. 'If you'll excuse me, there's a client over there I have to see . . . ' Her parting shot to Helen, 'I do hope you'll pick up some suitable 'little watercolours,' but I doubt you'll find them at my exhibition.' If there was any chance of Helen Lavalle wanting to buy any of her landscapes, she thought viciously, she'd make damn sure Derek trebled the price — no quadrupled it!

It was beginning to sink in that Ben was a married man — and a convicted felon — who hadn't seen fit to tell her either fact! Her heart felt leaden. The prison bit she could understand. Ben was a proud man, who would always carry it as his own dark secret, if that were possible. No wonder he'd hated the idea of a portait, and subsequent publicity. How many other people had recognised his picture, she wondered? It hardly mattered now, as he and Helen were going to live in France. It was doubtful whether anyone in the

Domaine de Lavalle area knew or cared about Ben's past.

It was the concealment of his marriage that hurt. She remembered his words the first night he'd come to the cottage. 'I was — once', implying something long ago in the past. And he'd dared to be censorious about her affair with Hugh!

'Are you Tamara? I just love this landscape. Can you tell me about it please?' An American woman buttonholed her eagerly, and led her over to one of her English Castle paintings. Tara smiled encouragingly, and started to tell the potential client all about Warwick Castle. After all, that's what she was there for. The fate of Ben's portrait could wait.

Kept occupied by a continual stream of enquiries and questions, she didn't see Helen Lavalle again, and it wasn't until half an hour before closing time that the crowd began to thin.

Bryn Evans, high on success, looked punch drunk. Derek couldn't conceal his delight at the way things had gone, and Tara wondered how she was going to get through the two remaining days of the show. She longed to plead illness, and head back to the sanctuary of Tamary Hollow.

Then she saw it. The last straw! 'Derek! You can't have. I told you, the portrait wasn't for sale.'

'You didn't say that, Tara. In any case, I've got an amazing price for it. Twice what I'd originally thought of asking. No quibbles either.' He looked proudly at the red sticker in the top right hand corner — the final proof of success. A sale!

'Who . . . ?' but Tara already knew the answer.

'Helen Lavalle bought it. I killed two birds with the one stone. Pre-empted all the fuss about showing it without permission, and made a huge profit for us. Tara, what's the matter?' One look at her stricken face told him he'd done the wrong thing. 'Tara,' he said again, 'was it so important to you? You'll do others.

Perhaps Ben Lavalle will sit again some time.'

'Derek — you have to get that portrait back for me. At any price. I don't care how you do it — just do it!'

10

Tara left London deeply disappointed. The exhibition had been a success, but it was a success which had lost its savour. Derek had promised he would do his best to retrieve the portrait but, gradually as the weeks went by at Tamary Hollow, that too mattered less and less.

To her growing dismay, the painting block persisted. After returning home, Tara had tried to work, and failed; the frustration of that failure was like a physical illness. A blight had attacked her creativity, and there was nothing she could do about it. Finally, she shut up the studio and waited, trying to stifle the black dog of fear that maybe her talent had deserted her for ever.

Somehow she had to fill the vacuum of time, and the renovation of the vineyard gave her a project. Before, it had provided a haven, a contrast to her career — now, it had to be more than that. In consultation with Tom, she planned the resurrection of the damaged vineyard, based on some of the ideas Ben had put forward.

'His plans do make sense, and I've been working to scale them down for Tamary. Ben's place sounds a lot bigger, from what you tell me.' Tom was enthusiastic.

'Yes.' Tara's response was short. She agreed. Ben's plans did make sense, but she couldn't bear to talk or think too much about him.

'Even so, it's ambitious. Mechanising the bottling, buying crops from smaller vineyards, expanding sales, more permanent staff — can you afford it all?'

'If you mention money once more, I'll sell up, and disappear from Tamary altogether,' Tara responded with mock severity. Ironically, Ben would, indirectly, be financing some of the improvements — from the sale of the portrait. Derek had told her there was now no chance that Helen Lavalle would re-sell. Briskly, she closed the file of plans. 'Right. We're going ahead, starting immediately. Come on Tom, let's go!'

★   ★   ★

Just a few days before Christmas, she called a halt to the cracking pace she'd set. In her present mood, she would have preferred to work throughout the holiday period, but naturally, the others didn't share her view.

Tamary Vineyard looked a vastly different place from the sleepy little collection of fields and sheds which it had been before the great storm. Brick buildings were under construction, land had been cleared for a new vine variety, and older vines restaked for training by a more modern method.

Part of her regretted the loss of the makeshift amateurism and rural charm that had characterised the place, but she philosophically accepted that this was how it would have to be.

There were invitations to spend Christmas with family and friends, but Tara refused, preferring complete seclusion, and a cutting off from the outside world. Then in total isolation, she promised herself she would return to the studio. And try to paint again.

Snow came to Devon early that year, and the village looked like an old fashioned Christmas card scene, crisp whiteness smoothing out all traces of the storm scars. Pushing herself, with an effort, into celebration mood on Christmas Eve, she gave a small party for her village friends and vineyard workers. Informal and friendly, it was a reminder of former days, but she found herself watching the clock, and was glad when her guests started to leave, some to go to midnight service, others to fill up their children's Christmas stockings. Try as she might, it was impossible for her to share the air of excited anticipation which surrounded her.

Tom lingered after everyone had

gone, insisting on helping to clear away. He seemed faintly anxious, as though he had something on his mind, and she prayed that he wasn't going to try and revive any romantic notions. Ostentatiously, she yawned. 'Thanks, Tom, that just about does it. I'm suddenly quite tired.'

'It was a good party.' Tom cleared his throat nervously. 'There's something I want to say, Tara.'

Her heart sank. 'It's a bit late . . . '

'Good heavens, it's Christmas Day already.' He glanced at the clock and relief beamed from his face, as he produced a large gift-wrapped parcel. He thrust it at her. 'So, I can give you this now. It's — it's just a thanks for staying with it! We're all grateful you've kept the vineyard, especially me, and if all goes well, Ginny and I can get engaged! That's what I wanted to tell you. She couldn't come tonight. Carol service, you know — she's leading soprano!'

Tara said thankfully. 'You and Ginny!

I never suspected, but I'm so glad.' Ginny was a student from the next village who'd frequently helped out at harvest times, and who'd been in love with Tom since she was a teenager. 'You played that close to your chest.' She laughed.

'Oh, well — er — you know . . . Go on, open the parcel.'

'You shouldn't have bought me anything — the vineyard's important to me too.' She put the package on the table and undid the wrappings. Then gasped.

'Tom, they're lovely!' Carefully, she lifted one of a dozen glasses to the light. Two sets of heavy lead crystal, six flutes, and six goblets. Beautiful enough, but what touched Tara's heart were the engravings. Each one represented a different growing stage of the vine, through the seasons, but common to all were the words 'TAMARY VINEYARD', and a delicate impression of the vineyard as it had been. A few practised strokes had exactly caught its old charm.

'Tom, they're absolutely beautiful. I'll treasure them for ever.'

'Thought you might like a reminder — of how things used to be,' he said gruffly. 'I'll be off now, I've kept you up long enough. Glad you like the glasses.'

'Like them — they're perfect! I'll use them specially for our own wine. A very happy Christmas to you, and to Ginny.' She went over to the door, where he was putting on his jacket, and hugged him gratefully.

'You're a good friend, Tom. I don't know what I'd have done without . . .'

They both froze at a sharp sound. 'What . . . ?'

'Ssh.' Tom still held her. 'I think there's someone out there — by the door.'

As he spoke, the latch clicked up, and the door slowly swung open. A tall figure was framed in the doorway, backed by whirling snow flakes.

'You!' Tara gasped in shocked amazement.

'Ben?' Tom's voice was uncertain as he moved hastily away from Tara.

'I was just . . . we were just . . . ' Tom floundered.

Ben smiled at them, stepped across the threshold, and closed the door. 'It's a cold night. Do you mind if I come in?' The gust of icy air he'd brought in with him, dissipated slowly. He saw the glasses, picked up one of them, and whistled. 'What beauties. Did you design them Tara?'

'No. Tom's idea. A Christmas present.' She answered automatically, stunned by Ben's totally unexpected appearance at Tamary Hollow in the early hours of Christmas morning. As realisation sunk in, her heart began to pound erratically. He looked younger, his beard had gone, and the gaunt look had totally vanished.

Tom said, 'It's a sort of thank-you, as well as a Christmas present. Tara's reconstructing the vineyards — the way you wanted — she's sunk a lot of money into all our futures.'

He sounded defensive. Ben said, 'So I see. Even in the snowstorm, it's impossible not to see the difference. So, what finally decided you to move with the times, Tara?'

He was very much at ease in the kitchen, and all the remembered hurts rose in her. She bit her lip. The last thing she wanted was for him to believe she had done it for him. Crushing the surge of joy that had raced in her blood when he'd appeared, she said, 'I really didn't have much choice. Anyway it's a bit late for you to show interest in Tamary — after leaving in such a hurry.'

'Not surprisingly,' he murmured evenly, looking directly at her. The tension between them began to rise.

Tom still stood uncomfortably by the door, looking anxiously from one to the other. 'Tara, I'd better be going.'

Before she could speak, Ben said quickly, 'Yes thanks, Tom, I do want to speak to Tara — in private.'

'Tom'll stay, if he wants to,' she flashed back.

'I'd better go, if that's all right with you, Tara? Shall I look in in the morning?'

'No. Christmas Day is for you and your family — and Ginny, of course. I'll see you after the holiday. And thanks again — for everything.'

Tom let himself out, and silence fell in the cosy room. It was Tara who broke it.

'Why have you come back?'

Ben moved towards her, his eyes noting the strain in hers, the tension at the corners of her mouth. His expression softened, and his hands came out to her.

'Isn't it obvious?' he murmured.

She moved back. 'Things have changed. Don't think you can just walk in in here and pick up where you left off.'

He shrugged, took off his coat, and dropped it on a chair. 'I haven't changed Tara, but there are things we have to sort out.'

'Such as?' she asked warily.

'Such as this!' He spoke hoarsely, and in one swift movement, took her in his arms, his lips hungrily searching hers. Her treacherous body leaped in joyful response to his, and her senses reeled as he kissed her passionately. For the moment it didn't matter that he was a married man — or a man with a past. Nothing mattered except Ben and what he meant to her.

When he raised his head, his arms remained around her. His voice was husky. 'I've thought of little else except you since the day I left. Your image has haunted me, but now I'm with you I love you even more than my imagination dreamed of.'

He bent to kiss her again, but with a desperate effort, Tara pulled away. She had to fight her own strength of feeling, and pride came to help her.

'No. You kept too many things from me — too many secrets. Your prison sentence — most of all, the fact that you still had a wife. You were here under false pretences.'

At that, Ben let her go. 'All right, if it's explanations you want, you'd better make us some coffee.' His mouth twitched in a crooked smile. 'And you'd better keep your distance. You're far too distracting.'

He sat down, and Tara, thankful for occupation to calm her own ragged breathing, busied herself with cups and coffee pot. Away from his persuasive arms, her resentment resurfaced. 'The fact you'd been to prison was your affair — but Helen? At least, you should have told me about her.'

'I did. That first night I came to supper. I told you, I was married once. Helen was my ex-wife, even then.'

'But she said . . . she told me you were going to be reconciled — live together in France. I got the impression . . . '

Ben broke in sharply. 'Helen is — was — always an expert at the art of giving the wrong impression. I admit I was in love with her years ago. I was young and she was beautiful, exciting, glamorous. Now I know, to my cost, she's beautiful, but shallow, and corrupt. What she did distorted my view of women. I took you to be of the same species, that first time, in the dusk outside your cottage, looking crazily inappropriate in your short skirt and high heels . . . just like her. How could I trust you? I couldn't trust anyone.'

The grim bitterness returned, and Tara's heart wrenched with pity. Her hands shook as she put a mug of coffee beside him. He took a sip, and stared at her sombrely. 'Have you the least idea what it's like — two years — locked away for a crime you didn't commit.'

'But, if you didn't, who . . . '

'My ex-wife, and ex-partner.' His voice was bitter, 'Between them, they transferred all our assets abroad. They concocted what seemed like a fool-proof plan. Me out of the way, blamed for their crime — and for them a life of luxury on a Caribbean island. It would have worked except that a leopard doesn't change its spots. Robert double-crossed Helen too. He dumped her and took off abroad. When I came out, I'd inherited the money from my aunt and I hired a top class firm of investigators. They've uncovered new evidence, which is now with the proper authorities. At last I can prove my innocence. But it's more important to me that you believe me Tara. You do see why I couldn't come to you before? I had to clear my name.' He looked at her intently, then reached out, and pulled her to him, nestled her in the crook of his arm, and kissed her lightly on the lips. Tracing the contours of her face with his fingers, he began to kiss her again with growing fervour.

Tara lifted her eyes. She could admit now, that this was the man she loved. But even as she watched his face, his expression changed to a frown. His voice, when he spoke, was accusing.

'But what about your secret, Tara? Why couldn't you trust me? The way you kept looking at me — I began to suspect you knew my identity. But you were so maddeningly evasive and secretive. Why couldn't you tell me about the protrait? It was unfair, and strictly unethical — Tamara!'

'Well, would you have agreed to sit for me?'

'You know I wouldn't! Any recognition, any publicity, would have alerted Helen — or the media.' Ben gave a short laugh. 'I didn't need that.'

'Do you know that she's bought the portrait, anyway — to put in your home she said.'

'She tried to use it as a weapon — she said she still loved me — after Robert had dumped her. The truth is that she found out I'd become wealthy. You must believe me, Tara, Helen's actions don't sway me in any way. She can never be anything to me again. I came back to Tamary Hollow to talk about you — us — in the hopes that we have a future together. But we have to be honest with each other first.'

'A future?'

Ben sighed, his frown disappeared,

and the dark eyes looked at her with liquid eloquence. 'Darling, have I to spell it out? You know how I feel about you — or do I have to show you?'

Tara closed her eyes, thinking he was going to kiss her. When she opened them again, he'd gone. The quiet kitchen was empty, with no trace of Ben, until she felt the cold blast of air as the door opened and he returned. He was carrying a large, flat package. Tara knew at once what it was. He held it out to her.

'Here. Your second Christmas present. From me — with all my love — forever.'

Tara eagerly reached out her hands to take back the portrait she'd painted with such pride and pleasure, but Ben held on to it. 'Oh no, you don't, it's not that easy. There's a condition attached to this gift.'

'Ben! What do you mean?'

'You have to take the original with it. I love you, Tara, and I'm asking you to marry me.' Just a hint of anxiety clouded his handsome face.

Tara couldn't bear it a moment longer. She went towards him with arms outstretched, her voice choked with happiness. 'Ben Lavalle, I love you, too. I think I always have, and I always will. Of course I'll marry you . . .'

Ben placed the portrait carefully on the floor and came to claim her. He looked intently into her eyes, and spoke softly. 'No more secrets, Tara, ever.'

'Never! I promise.'

Ben's kiss was the sweetest thing she'd experienced. Tara knew instinctively that they had, in mutual love, revealed their true identities to each other at last, and because of that she knew she would be able to paint again.

THE END

VISIONS OF THE HEART

Christine Briscomb

When property developer Connor Grant contracted Natalie Jensen to landscape the grounds of his large country house near Ashley in South Australia, she was ecstatic. But then she discovered he was acquiring — and ripping apart — great swathes of the town. Her own mother's house and the hall where the drama group met were two of his targets. Natalie was desperate to stop Connor's plans — but she also had to fight the powerful attraction flowing between them.

THE DOCTOR WAS A DOLL

Claire Vernon

Jackie runs a riding-school and, living happily with her father, feels no desire to get married. When Dr. Simon Hanson comes to the town, Jackie's friends try to matchmake, but he, like Jackie, wishes to remain single and they become good friends. When Jackie's father decides to remarry, she feels she is left all alone, not knowing the happiness that is waiting around the corner.

FINGALA, MAID OF RATHAY

Mary Cummins

On his deathbed, Sir James Montgomery of Rathay asks his daughter, Fingala, to swear that she will not honour her marriage contract until her brother Patrick, the new heir, returns from serving the King. Patrick must marry. Rathay must not be left without a mistress. But Patrick has fallen in love with the Lady Catherine Gordon whom the King, James IV, has given in marriage to the young man who claims to be Richard of York, one of the princes in the Tower.

ZABILLET OF THE SNOW

Catherine Darby

For Zabillet, a young peasant girl growing up in the tiny French village of Fromage in the mid-fourteenth century, a respectable marriage is the height of her parents' ambitions for her. But life is changing. Zabillet's love for a handsome shepherd is tested when she is invited to join the La Neige household, where her mistress, Lady Petronella, has plans for her grandson, Benet. And over all broods the horror of the Great Death that claims all whom it touches.

PERILOUS JOURNEY

Caroline Joyce

After the execution of Charles I, Louisa's Royalist father considers it too dangerous for her to stay in England and arranges for her to go to the Isle of Man with Armand de la Tremouille, the nephew of the island's Royalist Governor. Their ship is boarded by Parliamentarians who plan to sail for Ireland, but a storm causes them to be shipwrecked on the Calf of Man. Magnus Stapleton, the Parliamentarian chief, becomes infatuated with Louisa, but she has fallen in love with Armand.

THE GYPSY'S RETURN

Sara Judge

After the death of her cruel father, Amy Keene's step-brother and step-sister treated her just as badly. Amy had two friends, old Dr. Hilland and the washerwoman, Rosalind, with her fatherless child Becky. When Rosalind falls ill, Amy is entrusted with a letter to be given to Becky on her marriage. When the letter's contents are discovered, it causes Amy both mental and physical suffering and sets the seal of fate upon Rosalind's gypsy friend, Elias Jones.